SPIRIT FIGHTER

SPIRIT FIGHTER

Son of Angels
JONAH STONE

Book 1

JEREL LAW

THOMAS NELSON
Since 1798

NASHVILLE DALLAS MEXICO CITY RIO DE JANEIRO

Published in Nashville, Tennessee, by Tommy Nelson. Tommy Nelson is a registered trademark of Thomas Nelson, Inc.

Tommy Nelson® titles may be purchased in bulk for educational, business, fund-raising, or sales promotional use. For information, please e-mail SpecialMarkets@ThomasNelson.com.

Scripture quotations are from the New Century Version®. © 2005 by Thomas Nelson, Inc. Used by permission. All rights reserved; The New King James Version. © 1982 by Thomas Nelson, Inc. Used by permission. All rights reserved; the Holy Bible, New International Version®, NIV®. © 1973, 1978, 1984, 2011 by Biblica, Inc.™ Used by permission of Zondervan. All rights reserved worldwide. www.zondervan.com.

Library of Congress Cataloging-in-Publication Data

Law, Jerel.
    Spirit fighter / Jerel Law.
        p. cm. — (Son of angels ; bk. 1)
    Summary: Seventh-grader Jonah Stone discovers that he is one-quarter angel—his mother is the daughter of a human and a fallen angel—and when she is kidnapped, Jonah and his sister Eliza must try to rescue her, with the help of prayers and a guardian angel.
      ISBN 978-1-4003-1843-8 (pbk.)
      [1. Angels—Fiction. 2. Guardian angels—Fiction. 3. Christian life—Fiction. 4. Kidnapping—Fiction. 5. Adventure and adventurers—Fiction. 6. New York (N.Y.)—Fiction.] I. Title.
PZ7.L418365Sp 2011
[Fic]—dc23   2011023191

Printed in the United States of America

12 13 14 15 QG 6 5 4 3 2 1

For Susan,
my angel

CONTENTS

CONTENTS

PART I

BEGINNINGS

The Nephilim were on the earth in those days and also later.... These women gave birth to children, who became famous and were the mighty warriors of long ago.

Genesis 6:4 NCV

ONE

THE TRYOUT

Jonah's alarm blared in his left ear, but his eyes stayed shut and he didn't flinch, his left leg hanging over the edge of the top level of his bunk bed, a puddle of drool coming out of his mouth and onto his Star Wars pillowcase.

Just a few more minutes of sleep. That was all he needed.

Thump thump thump.

"Ungh . . . ," Jonah moaned.

Thump thump thump.

Jonah felt the board under his mattress move. He pulled the covers over his head and tried to ignore the frantic buzzing, knowing what his clock said without even having to look: 6:03 a.m. His least favorite time of the day. He'd slept horribly the last three nights, waking up each morning with the same fuzzy memory of a dream. Something about evil faces . . . howling wind . . . and angels.

The bunk beds began to creak and shake, and he knew that Jeremiah was not going to leave him alone. Even though Jeremiah was only seven years old (Jonah was thirteen), he was already catching up to his older brother in size. The bed bounced again, and from underneath the sheet Jonah felt the warm breath of a face about two inches away from his.

"Jonah!" Jeremiah said in a loud, raspy voice—his version of a whisper.

Jonah didn't move.

Jeremiah grabbed his older brother by the shoulders and shook. "Jonah! Get up! It's time for school!"

Jonah yanked the sheet down off his face.

"Jeremiah . . . ," he said, tired and cranky. But his brother was just sitting there grinning at him in his Scooby-Doo pajamas, breathing in his face.

The bedroom door opened. "Boys," came a girl's voice, "it's time to get up. We're going to be late for school if you don't start moving, you know."

Their eleven-year-old sister, Eliza, stood across the hallway, teasing her hair into place in front of a mirror on the wall. She was lanky like their mother, and she frowned behind her wire-rimmed glasses at a wild curl that wouldn't stay in place. Jonah launched his pillow at her, which she saw coming out of the corner of her eye and avoided just in time. It smacked harmlessly against the wall. Jeremiah fell back in the bed, laughing. Jonah drew his head back under the sheet for one more minute and let his mind wander.

Lately, Jonah's life had not gone as planned. Even though he was in seventh grade, he was still in the same school with Eliza and Jeremiah. Granger Community School had recently expanded to include students all the way from kindergarten to eighth grade, so he was stuck walking the halls knowing total embarrassment could be waiting around any given corner.

Two weeks ago Jonah was in the lunchroom when Jeremiah walked in and spotted him. He saw the wild look in his brother's eyes, which made him drop his cafeteria taco on his tray, splattering it all over his shirt, and murmur to himself in quiet humiliation, "Oh *no*."

He knew what was coming; he just couldn't stop it.

"JOOOOOONNNAAAAAHHHHH!"

His brother launched himself into a full-fledged sprint to come give him a bear hug. Two tables, eight lunch trays, and a very frightened Mrs. Clagmire were no match for his excitement, and they all went flying onto the floor.

And then, just the other day, the principal made this announcement over the school intercom:

> Congratulations to our very own fifth grader Eliza Stone for her recent accomplishments. She won first place in the science fair, the blue ribbon at the Math-letes Regional Competition for the Academically Advanced, and the gold medal for the local chapter of Whiz-Kid Computer Programmers International—all in the same week! Brilliant, Eliza! We at Granger Community School are privileged to have such a gifted student in our midst. Bravo!

Since then, Zack Smellman and his bully buddies had taken every chance they could to remind him that his little sister was smarter than he was. Which was funny, coming from a group of guys still taking third-grade math.

Jonah sighed loudly and finally forced himself to climb down from the top bunk. He pulled his clothes on quickly in the dark.

Still half-asleep, he staggered down the stairs, landing in a chair at the weathered wooden table beside Jeremiah, who was halfway through his bowl of Frosted Flakes. Eliza was already finished with breakfast and waiting by the door impatiently, her book bag strapped tightly to her back.

"Mom, why do Jeremiah and I *have* to share a room?"

Jonah's mom smiled at him sleepily, pushed the wispy blond hair from her face, and planted a kiss on his forehead. Even in her rumpled bathrobe, Eleanor Stone was stunning. Tall, with wide shoulders, hair pulled back in a ponytail, she commanded attention wherever she was.

"Haven't we been through this before, dear?" she said, running her fingers through his thick, black hair. "We only have three bedrooms, and Eliza's a girl. She needs a room to herself."

Jonah sighed. He imagined what it would be like to have a room to himself, where none of his stuff got bothered and broken, where he could lock the door and play video games or read a comic book without being pestered.

"What would you like for breakfast, hon?"

"Cereal is fine," he said, snapping out of his fantasy. He shook the flakes into a chipped green bowl while she poured milk from a plastic jug. "Where's Dad?"

"He had a late meeting at the church last night, so he's sleeping in this morning."

Jonah nodded, crunching on his cereal slowly. His dad was the pastor of All Souls United Methodist Church in Peacefield, and late-night meetings were a regular thing.

"Don't forget your basketball shoes and shorts, dear," she said, using one hand to try to tame his mane of hair. "Tryouts are today, remember?"

It was often easy for Jonah to forget things, like homework (he forgot to do two English assignments last week) or chores (his parents had started attaching brightly colored notes to his tennis shoes and video games), but forget that basketball tryouts for the middle school boys' team at Granger Community School were today? It was all he had thought about for weeks. True, he was a little shorter than most of the boys in his class, but he was fast, and he had been practicing in his driveway every single day for the last month. He was ready.

"Yeah, Mom, I know," he said, munching a little quicker, suddenly feeling more awake.

His mom lifted his chin with her finger and looked at him with her bright green eyes. "Just know that whatever happens, your father and I are very proud of you."

Jeremiah suddenly hopped up and wrapped his arms around Jonah's neck, tightly squeezing as he talked, so hard that Jonah coughed up some of his breakfast. "Yeah, Jonah, we are *proud-of-you!*"

Eliza still stood at the door, her arms crossed and scowling. She wore a pink, sparkly blouse and a black skirt with leggings. Even Jonah had noticed she was dressing differently this year. No more sweatpants and raggedy T-shirts. But she was still his little sister. "Yes, yes, we are all *so* proud of you, big brother," she said sarcastically. "Now can we get going, please? You're going to make us miss the bus!"

They had to run to the bus stop, but they made it. In almost no time the bus pulled up to a campus of large, one-story brick buildings. Granger Community School sprawled out in every direction, connected by an intricate spiderweb of cracking concrete walkways.

Jeremiah stood at the bottom of the bus steps waiting patiently for his big brother. "Come on, Jonah, take me to class."

When school started, their mom made Jonah promise he would walk his brother to his class. But that was four weeks ago. *Shouldn't you know your way to your own room by now?* Jonah thought as he looked down at Jeremiah.

Jonah sighed, knowing it wasn't worth the argument. "Fine. But I'm not holding your hand."

He dropped his head a little lower as he walked beside his brother, who happened to be skipping. As a seventh grader, Jonah knew nothing good was going to come from people seeing him walk around every morning with a little kid wearing a Scooby-Doo backpack.

Jonah dropped Jeremiah off at his classroom and then hurried to the seventh-grade hallway, entering his first class just as the bell rang.

"Nice kicks, Stone. Been shopping at the Goodwill store again?"

The boys sitting around Zack Smellman's desk snorted, and he grinned at Jonah with his arms folded.

Gritting his teeth, Jonah reminded himself that the first day of basketball tryouts started this afternoon. Smellman was not going to get the best of him today.

So he didn't let it bother him later that morning when he got back his science test and only scored a seventy-eight. He was not shaken when his math teacher gave the class two hours of extra homework. All he could think about was what was going to happen on the basketball court.

Finally, mercifully, the clock struck three. His stomach was doing somersaults, but he was ready. He knew it.

With his gym clothes on and basketball shoes laced up, he took the floor with the other boys. Thirty-nine, to be exact, going out for just twelve spots. He glanced at them nervously, sizing up the competition. Most of them seemed bigger and stronger than he was.

Jonah grabbed a ball to warm up and started taking shots, trying not to let any bad thoughts seep into his brain. He began with free throws. He was really good at these. *Clang. Clang. Clang.* Three in a row went bouncing off the rim. The fourth hammered off the backboard and didn't even touch the rim at all. At home he would make three out of four, at least. What was going on? Suddenly his lunch felt like it was about to come up.

Coach Martin Nelderbaum, or "Coach Marty," as he told everybody to call him, was the physical education instructor at the school. He said he had played basketball in high school, but Jonah couldn't see how. Coach Marty almost had the proportions of a basketball himself, with a huge belly that hung out from the bottom of his way-too-small gray gym shirt. He practically yelled every word that came out of his mouth.

"Hello! My name is Coach Marty! Today is the first day of Middle School Boys Basketball Tryouts! You are mine for the next hour and a half, and you will do whatever I say! Now, don't take this the wrong way, but a bunch of you are NOT GOING TO MAKE THIS TEAM!"

He had to pause there to take a few breaths, exhausted already from his own scream-talking.

"Try your hardest! I will be looking for the best twelve players on this floor! I want to see one hundred percent effort from each of you!" Jonah zoned out a little when Coach Marty went on like this for ten more minutes, even though he was determined to pick up any last-minute pointers he could—apparently it looked like he would need them. Finally, Coach Marty instructed everybody to get in a line in front of the basket, and the tryouts were officially underway.

No one tried harder than Jonah. But in the running drills, he was one of the last to finish the wind sprints. He missed three out of the five layups he attempted in the layup drill. His free throws bounced off the basket like there was an invisible cover on it. When he lined up to take three-point shots, only one out of four even hit the rim. The rest totally missed the goal. One of them even hit Coach Marty in the stomach when he wasn't looking. He grunted, glared at Jonah, and tossed the ball to the next guy.

Jonah watched as the coach stared at him with one eye while writing furiously on his clipboard. He swallowed hard. Was he writing something about him?

It was a miserable tryout. He couldn't stay out of his own way. But Jonah reminded himself that at least there were two more days to prove himself. Coach Marty gathered the boys in the center of the court and yelled at them again, "Saw a lot of great stuff out there today, men! For the most part, you boys did great! Same time, same place tomorrow afternoon! Now, hit the locker room!"

The tired boys were staggering away from mid-court when Coach Marty, still staring down at his clipboard, barked, "Stone, comma, Jonah! A word with you, son!"

As the others left, Coach Marty put his arm around Jonah's shoulder and spoke in a slightly more normal volume for the first time that day. "Son," he said, sounding only a little less like the human bullhorn he was before, "do you play any other sports?"

Jonah stared at him for a minute, not understanding the question. When he opened his mouth, all that came out was a sputter of words.

"Well . . . not really . . . I . . . basketball is . . . my . . ."

Coach Marty patted his shoulder and nodded sadly.

"Listen, son, I've seen a lot of great basketball players in my day, and I can confidently say that after watching you practice today, basketball is not your sport."

The words hung in the air, and Jonah felt like the coach had suddenly begun speaking a foreign language. *Not. Your. Sport.* What did he mean? Coach Marty saw the confusion on his face and took a more direct route this time.

"I don't think you need to come back tomorrow, Stone," the coach said gruffly. "I've seen enough. You're not going to make the team."

He patted Jonah on the shoulder hard, twice.

"Truth hurts sometimes, kid. But don't worry. There are plenty of other sports to play." Then, as if he had just had the greatest idea ever, he said, "Ever thought about badminton?"

And with that, he walked off the court, leaving Jonah standing there alone, mouth hanging open.

"Basketball is not your sport." The words started to sink in. *"Ever thought about badminton?" "Not. Your. Sport."* Jonah turned and walked slowly back into the locker room. All the boys were laughing loudly, bragging about all the shots they made in the try-out. Jonah shuffled quietly to his locker, grabbed his stuff, and made a beeline for the door. He just wanted to be invisible.

He tore across the gym floor and pushed the metal double doors open, slamming one of them hard against the brick wall on the outside of the building. How could this happen? How could he have played so badly? And how could Coach Marty have asked him not to come back tomorrow? His legs began to move faster. He was not sure where he was running, but he just needed to go. To get away from everything, from the gym, the other guys. From everyone.

Jonah found himself on the empty soccer field behind the school. He slowed down and began to catch his breath. Suddenly the words his dad had said a million times popped into his head.

"If you're ever stuck, pray. Trust me, it will all work out."

He sighed heavily as he brought himself to a halt and slipped his gym bag from his shoulder, standing in the middle of the field and leaning over with his hands on his knees. "God, it's Jonah," he said, and with that, the words began to erupt. "I know You are there, and I know You love me. But I don't know what to do. Things aren't great right now. I can't believe what just happened at the basketball tryout. I know I haven't been getting much sleep the past couple nights, but am I really that bad? Everyone thinks I'm a loser. I'm . . . I'm not good at . . . anything . . ."

Tears began to form in his eyes and then run hotly down his face. He wiped them on his shirtsleeve, but that didn't help them stop. Instead, his shoulders began to shake and his chest heaved as he cried. He stood there until the tears finally dried up.

"God, can You help me? Can You show me what to do? Can You just fix this?"

His dad was fond of calling God *Elohim*, one of His names from the Bible, which in the ancient Hebrew language meant "Strong One." He also loved to tell Jonah and his brother and sister that praying was the most powerful thing any human could do. And that Elohim listened to them—and that if they would listen back, He would speak. But the truth was, neither Jonah—or his dad, as far as he knew—had ever heard God's voice. Maybe it was just something his dad was supposed to say. He was a pastor, after all. It was his job to believe that stuff.

Jonah looked up at the sunny sky, hoping for an answer, but

all he heard were a few birds chirping in the distance. And even they grew silent. He shrugged his shoulders and began to walk off the field. What did he expect? For God to show up on the field and turn him into LeBron James? What a joke.

He suddenly felt his anger welling up again, at the coach, at himself, at everybody, and he clenched his teeth. A stray soccer ball was on the field in front of him, and without thinking, he charged it, kicking it at the soccer goal as hard as he could.

Then the strangest thing happened.

The ball bounced—no, flew—no, *rocketed* off of his foot. It went up, higher than the goal, higher than the treetops, and kept rising, like it was shot out of a cannon. Jonah's mouth dropped open as he watched the ball fly up, up, up, so far into the sky that it was a speck within a few seconds.

Then it was gone.

Spotting another abandoned ball, he looked around to see if anyone had seen what had just happened. No one was in sight, so he concentrated on the ball in front of him, ran toward it, and swung his leg.

The ball shot off like a rocket again, blasting over the forest behind the school and—at least it *looked* like it—tearing a hole through a lone white cloud in the sky. Then it disappeared.

Jonah pushed his fingers through his matted hair. He had never seen anybody do what he just did. He was pretty sure that a professional soccer player couldn't do that. So how did he, a thirteen-year-old kid who had just gotten kicked out of basketball tryouts for not being good enough, kick a soccer ball over the trees and out of sight?

What is going on? He stood staring at the sky, almost in a trance, as his mind churned.

Finally, he glanced down at his watch. He was late for his ride home. He grabbed his gym bag and quickly made his way around to the front of the gym, still shaking his head and looking at his foot.

TWO

A LITTLE BACKYARD
FOOTBALL

Eleanor Stone was waiting for her son in a rusty white Subaru station wagon in the pick-up lane in front of the school. Jonah climbed quietly into the car.

"How'd it go?" she asked, looking at him in the rearview mirror as she pulled away.

His mind was stuck on what had just happened on the soccer field, and it took him a few seconds to remember that she was asking about the basketball tryouts.

"Not great," he said, and he told her all about it, how bad he had done, and the talk Coach Marty had with him afterward. He saw his mother's eyes flash in the mirror.

"He told you not to come back?" she said loudly, slamming the brakes and sending Jonah lurching toward the front seat. "That's it! We're turning around. No one is going to treat—"

"Mom, please! You can't go back," Jonah said, cringing as

he pictured his mother yelling and shaking her finger in Coach Marty's face, and what Zack Smellman—and probably half the student body—would have to say about it later. "Everyone will see us, everyone will know that my mom came in and talked to the coach. Just . . . leave it alone."

"Jonah . . . ," she started to protest again, but she saw the look on his face and just pressed her lips into a tight line.

The rest of the ride home he stared out the window in silence. He sensed his mom's eyes watching him in the mirror but ignored them. He didn't feel like talking. The tryouts were one thing. But what happened with the soccer ball . . . it was just off-the-charts weird.

He wondered if he could do it again.

Because if he could, then maybe he could do more than just kick a soccer ball really far. His brain was telling him it must have been a trick ball, or some kind of optical illusion, maybe even something he only *thought* he saw after not getting a good night's sleep. But he began to feel a nervous excitement. Like somehow he was on the verge of something big. Then his mind continued to circle back to the awful tryout, reminding him of how much of a loser he was.

Jonah needed time to think.

When he got home, he immediately went to his room and locked the door behind him. Snapping on his headphones and plugging them into his portable video game player, he popped in a game and lost himself in a world of spaceships, force fields, and laser beams.

After a couple hours alone in his room, Jonah was ready to talk. He headed downstairs to his dad's study. Jonah peered through the glass-paned door and saw his dad inside, back turned to him, facing one of the three massive walls of books.

Books of all colors and sizes covered the walls. The desk was stacked high with piles of opened ones—dictionaries, Bibles, massive tomes in Greek and Hebrew. Some lay open; others were precariously balanced on top of each other in various places around the room. Jonah walked in and plopped himself down in his dad's squeaky old desk chair.

Benjamin Stone was so focused on finding a book that he didn't hear his son come in. Standing on his tiptoes, he reached up for a large encyclopedia, the overhead light shining brightly off the bald spot on his head as he stretched. Jonah's mom could have reached it easily, but his dad was short, just like him. After edging the book off the bookshelf with his finger and almost dropping it on his head, he finally had it. Pushing his glasses up his nose, he turned around as he searched the pages of the volume.

Jonah couldn't resist. He coughed loudly.

"Oh!" His father looked up and jumped at the same time, dropping his book. It landed on his foot. "Ow!"

Jonah smirked. "Hi, Dad."

"Son! You're going to give me a heart attack," his dad said, picking up the book and rubbing his foot. He came around the desk and held out his hand high, and Jonah instinctively slapped it in a high-five—their daily greeting. Benjamin sat down on the corner of his desk.

"Your mom told me about basketball tryouts," he said quietly. "Want to tell me about it?"

Jonah shrugged and spun around in the chair, not saying anything. It was official: he was terrible at basketball and he was never going to get another chance to prove himself. What was the point of talking about it?

His dad's face was mostly beard and glasses, but behind those were bright, blue eyes that blinked at him softly.

"I guess I can't make you talk about it, Jonah. But if you decide you want to discuss it, we can do that."

"I know," Jonah sighed, still spinning.

Then he stopped. "Dad, something really, really weird happened today."

"At the tryout?"

"No," said Jonah. "Afterward. And you're not going to believe me when I tell you about it."

Benjamin set the book down on the desk and cocked his head to the side, looking intently at his son.

"Try me."

Jonah took a deep breath, and launched rapid-fire into the story. He was sure that his dad would talk some sense into him. He would explain to him how he must have been imagining things, or tell him about some new high-tech soccer ball that had just come out. Offer some kind of explanation. His father's mouth hung open, and Jonah paused, waiting for whatever cool-headed advice his father would be sure to provide. But he didn't say a word.

"You don't believe me," Jonah finally said, feeling the anger well up inside him again.

"No, no"—his dad waved his hand in the air—"it's not that. It's just . . . well . . . come outside with me."

Jonah followed him out to the backyard. It was beginning to get dark, but there was still a little daylight left. Even though their house was small, they had a great backyard that met up with a large pond.

His father walked over to the small storage shed and leaned

inside, rummaging around, until he came out with something in his hands and a curious smile on his face.

"Here," he said. "Throw this." He tossed a football at him. Jonah caught it and squeezed it in his hands.

"To you?" he asked, and cocked his arm back toward his dad.

"No," Benjamin said, unable now to contain the excitement in his voice, "over there."

He motioned toward the other side of the water. Jonah blinked.

"Over there?" he said. "Across the pond?"

His dad nodded and pointed at a house in the distance. "At that blue house."

"But, Dad, what if it breaks a window?"

"Don't worry about that!" he said eagerly. "Just throw it. As hard as you can."

Jonah looked at the house. It was easily two and a half lengths of a football field away. Spreading his fingers across the laces, he gripped the ball firmly in his right hand. He took a few steps, drew his arm back, and threw.

The football took off just like the soccer balls had. It tore through the air over the pond. It went over the water, cleared the house by fifty feet, and disappeared from sight.

Benjamin Stone grabbed Jonah in a big bear hug as he broke into a fit of laughter. This made Jonah start to smile, and then chuckle a little. Before he knew it, they were both hugging and laughing so hard that Jonah was getting a stomachache.

"Amazing, Jonah! Absolutely amazing!" Benjamin finally said, and quickly he jogged back to the storage shed. This time he pulled out two old baseballs and a softball. Jonah threw each of these, with the same result. Each time, his father said something like "Wow!" or "Incredible!" or "Unbelievable!"

Finally, after they had both calmed down and Jonah's arm was starting to hurt a little, his father looked at him, now quite serious, and asked, "Jonah, did anything else happen right before you did this? Did you tell me everything that you remember?"

Jonah thought for a minute. "I prayed. Out loud," he said. "Because that's what you always tell me to do when things don't go the way they are supposed to."

A proud smile flickered across Benjamin's lips, but he let him continue.

"I just asked Elohim for help. I asked Him to fix it."

His dad nodded his head thoughtfully. "I think we should share this with your mother. The three of us need to have a little chat tonight."

Something in his dad's voice made Jonah shiver as they walked back inside.

THREE

THE NEPHILIM

Benjamin sent Eliza and Jeremiah up to bed early, despite their protests, and asked Jonah to sit at the kitchen table. Then he pulled his wife aside into the study, away from Jonah, and they began to talk in low whispers.

Jonah moved a little closer to see if he could overhear anything, but they were speaking too softly. Finally, his parents came back in and sat down, his dad placing his Bible on the table.

"Jonah," his father began, "like I said, there is something we need to discuss with you."

"What is it?" Jonah said, on the edge of his seat. His parents both seemed very nervous, and he felt like he was going to explode with curiosity.

His mother looked at him and swallowed hard before she spoke. "Jonah, you are not entirely human. You're *mostly* human, just not . . . *totally*."

She paused, and they both took shaky sips of coffee, watching Jonah's reaction and letting the words sink in.

"Not totally human? What in the world does that mean?"

"Well," she said, gathering herself. "Try not to be alarmed, son, but you are actually part . . . *angel*."

Jonah's head started to spin. Try not to be alarmed? She must be joking. That was the only explanation he could come up with. She was getting ready to burst out laughing, any second now.

"You're kidding, right?" Jonah asked. But neither one of them was smiling.

"No, we're not joking," his dad said. "We are entirely serious."

Jonah breathed in sharply. "I'm . . . *part angel*? Mom, Dad . . . seriously?"

His father glanced at Eleanor, and she nodded. "You are one-quarter angel, to be exact. You are what's known as a *quarterling*. We suspected that there would come a day when there would be something . . . unique . . . about you that would present itself. We just didn't think it would be so soon . . ."

Eleanor put her hand firmly on Benjamin's arm as he took an extra large gulp of coffee.

"Jonah," his mom said, "I need you to listen and accept what we are telling you. This is a very, very serious thing. And very real. Now, you and your brother and sister never knew my parents. And what your father and I have always told you is—"

"—that they died before we were born," Jonah said, jumping in to finish her sentence. "You never told us anything else. So you're saying . . . there's a lot more to it than that?"

"Yes, there is," she said calmly. "We wanted you to grow up with as normal a childhood as possible, so we never told you about them. Or me, for that matter. *Or you*."

Eleanor glanced at Benjamin again, and he continued this

time. "In order to understand who you are, you need to know the truth about your family. Your grandmother, Francine, was a lonely, troubled woman. Always searching for something, but never finding what she needed. What only Elohim could give her, of course. But sadly, she never turned to Him. Instead, she let someone else into her life. A man who called himself Victor Grace."

Eleanor grimaced at the coffee circling around in her cup.

"Victor was very handsome. Very charming. He took his time and swept her off her feet. She was in love and was fully convinced that the feeling was mutual. When Victor asked her to marry him, Francine of course said yes. But even though she had always wanted a big family wedding, Francine didn't invite anyone at all to the ceremony. Looking back, it's clear to see that he pulled her away from all of her friends and family, one by one, until he was the only person in her life. She did whatever he asked her to do."

"So they got married," Eleanor continued. "But after their wedding night, he disappeared. When she woke up in the morning, he had vanished. My mother didn't know where he had gone. She never heard from him again. But a few weeks later, she discovered she was pregnant."

"With a baby she would name Eleanor," his dad said with a slight smile, gently tucking a stray wisp of hair behind her ear before turning back to face his son. "When Victor left, it destroyed Francine. She had no faith, no friends or family, nothing to build a life on anymore. This turned her into a very bad mother, who was not very kind to her daughter. Especially when she discovered that her little girl was not so . . . normal."

"I began to do things that other five-year-olds couldn't do," Eleanor said, her eyes distant and sad. "When I was young, it would happen because I was angry. The first thing I remember doing was smashing a metal teakettle. It was a beautiful day, and I wanted to go outside and play. My mother was sitting on the couch, staring vacantly outside like she sometimes did. She refused to take me and wouldn't let me go by myself. There was a metal teapot on the table, and I got so mad that without thinking, I grabbed it and crushed it with my bare hands. Mother wouldn't let me play outside for a month."

She laughed softly. "I was just five years old. I didn't know how I had done it; I just did it. But it began to happen more often, at first whenever I would get angry, but along the way I began to discover that if I became very, very focused, I could learn to control what I did."

Jonah interrupted now. "So you're saying that I'm like that too? That I have these powers because I'm a . . . what did you call it, Dad?"

"A quarterling," his father said.

"So that means that my grandfather—"

"—was an angel. Yes," said Benjamin, finishing the sentence. "But listen closely, Jonah. There's more. We believe that your grandfather was a particular *kind* of angel. He was one of the Fallen."

Jonah sat back in his chair now, rubbing his eyes with the palms of his hands. Kicking soccer balls way too far . . . angels . . . quarterlings . . . the Fallen . . . it was all too much.

"But you have that picture of him, Mom, and he looks just like any other guy . . . well, for a guy back *then*, anyway," Jonah said, trying to make sense of everything they were telling him. She nodded and reached over, opening up a kitchen drawer. Pulling out a faded black-and-white photograph, she placed it on the table. It was a picture of a young couple holding each other closely. The woman was gazing up at the man with a huge smile on her face. The man was grinning confidently at the camera, a dark goatee on his chin, wearing a stylish brown suit and matching hat.

"This is the only picture I have of my parents," she said, her voice cracking as she outlined her mother's face with her finger.

"Jonah, I know this is a lot to take in," his father said, "but the sooner you can accept it, the better. We have kept these things hidden from you on purpose, but now it seems that Elohim Himself is ready for you to know."

"How do you know that?" Jonah asked.

"Well," said Benjamin, "I think that He answered your prayer today. You prayed right before you kicked that ball. For some reason that only He knows right now, He chose that moment to begin to reveal who you really are. To begin to show you how special Jonah Stone actually is."

But that's just it, Jonah thought. *I'm not special. Haven't any of you been paying attention to the last thirteen years of my life? There's nothing special about Jonah Stone.*

Another question popped into his head. "What about all of those athletes who pray for Him to give them strength and help them win their game right before they play, and then they go out and get creamed? Why do some prayers get answered, and others don't?"

His dad took a sip of coffee and smiled from behind his mug. "Elohim is Elohim."

It was one of his dad's favorite phrases. He tended to use it when there was not a simple explanation for something, and usually it frustrated Jonah. Like when an important soccer game got rained out. Or even when something really bad happened, like an earthquake on the other side of the world, or a flood that left people homeless. But for the first time, he caught a new glimpse of what his dad meant. Maybe Elohim really did have His own reason for the timing of this right now. Jonah just didn't know what it was.

"So you said my grandfather was—"

"One of the Fallen," Eleanor said. "He is a fallen angel."

Jonah thought for a minute. "Why did you say *is*?"

"Angels are eternal, Jonah," said his dad. "They were created by Elohim, and they never die. Somewhere, Victor Grace is still very much alive."

"I thought that angels and all of that stuff were just a story," Jonah said. "You know, like a fairy tale. I believe in Elohim and in the Bible, but I thought angels were something people made up. Floating around on clouds and playing harps and stuff. Do they do that?"

His mom and dad laughed. "Not exactly," his father said. "Angels are some of the most powerful creatures in the universe. Elohim created them to be in the service of His kingdom. But some of them—the Bible says about one-third—decided they didn't want to serve under Elohim's rule anymore. One of them even thought he could be better than Elohim."

Eleanor continued gravely, "A great battle took place. Michael, the leader of the angelic army, brought his forces to battle against the great deceiver, the angel who led the rebellion. He has been known by many names—Satan, Lucifer, the Prince of Darkness— but among angels he is known as Abaddon, the accuser. After a violent struggle, Michael threw Abaddon down to the earth, along with those Abaddon had convinced to fight with him. They are known as the Fallen, and they roam this earth, doing their master's bidding, still waging war against Elohim and His forces."

"Your father was a fallen angel," Jonah repeated, still not sure that he could bring himself to believe what he was hearing.

"Yes," Eleanor said, slowly tracing the rim of her coffee mug. "One who wanted a child."

"Why would one of the Fallen want a kid?"

Benjamin began to turn the pages of his Bible. "You are a quarterling, Jonah. What do you think that makes your mother?"

"I guess that means she is half angel," Jonah said. Then he looked thoughtfully at his father. "Dad, are *you* . . . ?"

His dad laughed. "Oh, I can assure you, I am entirely human. Your mom can vouch for this too. But you are right: she is half angel." He gazed at her. "Although she'll always be one hundred percent angel to me."

"Benjamin, stay focused," she said, but smiled as he began leafing through his Bible again.

"Ah, here it is," he said, fingering the right page. "Genesis 6:4 explains that the children of supernatural beings who had married human women became famous heroes and warriors. They were called nephilim and lived on the earth at that time and—as we have ample proof here at this table—even later."

He put his finger on the verse and turned it around for Jonah to see. Jonah read it several times slowly until he felt like he had the gist of the passage.

"So Mom is a . . . how do you say it?"

"*Nephilim*, pronounced *NE-fi-lim*," his dad said slowly. "The Bible says that angels came down and married women and had offspring by them. These offspring were known as nephilim. As you can see, the Bible says that they were quite extraordinary."

"Famous heroes and warriors," Jonah said, rereading the

passage. "Cool." He cocked his head and looked at his mom for a minute. "But . . ."

"I think one day you'll learn to recognize that there is something special about everyone, dear," she said, smiling.

Suddenly two distinct memories flashed across Jonah's mind. One from a few years ago, on a New York street. A man tried to grab his mom's purse and run. But suddenly, instead of a quick getaway, he was on the ground, dazed. Eleanor had him pinned to the sidewalk and was calmly lecturing him while they waited for the police to arrive.

The other was from last summer. It was of his mom crossing the finish line of the annual Peacefield marathon in first place. He remembered how odd it was that she hadn't even broken a sweat, and how it seemed like she had slowed down at one point just to let the fastest guy catch up. At the time, he couldn't understand why she had politely declined the invitation to run in the famous New York Marathon.

"And Eliza and Jeremiah?"

Benjamin nodded. "They are quarterlings too."

"But none of this answers why a fallen angel would want to have a child."

Benjamin and Eleanor looked at each other uncertainly.

"So far, the answer to that question remains a mystery," Benjamin said slowly.

Eleanor stood up from the table and kissed Jonah on the forehead. "And I believe that's quite enough new information for now. It's time for this young man to go to bed."

"Just one more thing for tonight," said Benjamin. "I know you have many more questions about this, Jonah, more than we can possibly answer. There is much we do not know, and there are many men and women wiser about these things than your parents. Now that you have learned these things about yourself, now that Elohim has begun to reveal who you really are, I want to make sure you grasp the most important thing. It is going to start to become much clearer to you that life is not what you thought it was. We told you there was a great battle between the angels of Elohim and the Fallen. Well, that battle still rages today. Elohim does not intend for us to be ignorant of it, nor does He wish that we are simply casual observers."

Benjamin looked intently into his son's eyes. "He intends for us to fight."

Jonah sat back in his chair, lost in thought. But his dad stood up from the table too.

"Your mom's right," he said, rubbing the top of his son's head. "They'll be plenty of time for more of this later. Right now, it's time for bed."

Reluctantly, still wanting answers, Jonah climbed the stairs to his room. Jeremiah was already curled up in bed, his sleepy eyes still half-open.

"G'night, Jonah," he said, managing a half smile, and rolled over toward the wall.

"Good night, Jeremiah," said Jonah. He climbed up to the top bunk and tried to slow his mind down enough to get some sleep, having little doubt what he would dream about tonight. In the center of his swirling brain, one thought continued to dominate.

This is all real.

Elohim, he finally prayed, *I don't even know where to start. Am I really part angel? A quarterling? All I can say is, I am going to need You to help me figure all of this out. Deal?*

Suddenly, he had an idea. Jumping back down, he grabbed his

raggedy-edged Bible from his desk, along with his small reading light. He climbed back in bed, pulled the covers over his head, and thumbed back to the index, searching the *As.*

"Ananias, Andrew, Angel . . . there we go."

There were dozens of places in the Bible that mentioned angels. He flipped over to the first one that caught his eye.

"Second Corinthians 11:14," he whispered to himself, ". . . for Satan himself masquerades as an angel of light." He didn't like the sound of that. He quickly moved to another passage, listed in the notes of his Bible.

"Hebrews 13:2," he said, turning the pages until he found it. "Do not forget to show hospitality to strangers, for by so doing some people have shown hospitality to angels without knowing it." His mom and dad were always inviting people over for dinner, mostly from the church. Maybe he had sat across the table from an angel without even knowing it.

One more caught his attention, Revelation 12:7: "Then war broke out in heaven. Michael and his angels fought against the dragon, and the dragon and his angels fought back."

Jonah studied this passage for a long time, trying to imagine the battle. Michael, the warrior angel, with his troops, fighting against the rebellious fallen ones and their leader, the dragon. Jonah knew this was probably another name for the chief of the Fallen himself. Abaddon.

He pulled the covers off his head and stared at the ceiling until his eyes grew tired, thinking about everything he had heard and read tonight. The fake glowing stars he had stuck on the ceiling when he was five were still there. And all he could see were angels swooping around them in perfect figure eights.

FOUR

A BULLY AFTER SCHOOL

I am one-quarter angel.

There's a battle going on between good and evil.

I have supernatural powers.

Those were the thoughts Jonah awoke to. He pulled on his jeans in the dark. *Are these Dad's?* Flipping on the light, he looked at himself in the mirror. No, they were his jeans. They were just two inches shorter than the day before.

Weird. Did I actually grow taller overnight?

All he could think about that day was his conversation with his parents. When he awoke from a daydream during math class and found himself staring at a poster that said FRACTIONS ARE FUN!, he wondered if he could use his super-strength to throw a pencil so hard it would go straight through the wall.

He was on the way to catch his bus after school when he heard voices ahead around the corner, laughing loudly. Looking down the alleyway between two buildings, he caught a glimpse of a group of boys. Three kids were standing in front of one smaller boy, pushing him against the brick wall. They had him surrounded. Jonah immediately recognized the ringleader as Zack Smellman. Beside him were two of his friends, Peter Snodgrass and Carl Fong.

Smellman had his long index finger pointed right between the small boy's eyes, a boy with dreadlocked hair Jonah vaguely recognized as a fifth grader. He looked terrified, on the verge of tears.

Jonah's first reaction was to keep on walking. He didn't need one more thing to worry about right now.

But the boy saw him as he was about to pass. In his face, with tears about to spill, Jonah saw a look of sheer terror. And then something inside Jonah welled up, overtaking his desire to ignore what was happening.

It was an irresistible feeling, almost like a voice, telling him to walk into the alley. He found himself taking a step in, out of the sunlight and into the shadows.

"What are you guys doing?" he asked. His voice cracked, and inside he kicked himself for sounding so wimpy.

"*What are you guys doing?*" Zack mimicked as Snodgrass and Fong snorted. He raised his voice. "Get outta here, Stone! We're just taking care of some business with our good friend here."

Smellman was at least eight inches taller than Jonah, and Fong was just a little shorter than that but must have been twice as heavy. Snodgrass was Jonah's height but built like a bulldozer.

Yesterday, Jonah *would* have gotten out of there. But not today. Something compelled him into the alleyway. The fear in the boy's face. And something else. He had to admit, he was curious to see what he could do with his new power.

"How about letting him go?" Jonah's voice was louder now, and steadier, the confidence in it surprising even him.

Zack stopped pushing the boy against the wall and turned to

face Jonah, Snodgrass and Fong right behind him. At least he had their attention. But now he had to figure out what to do next.

"Stone," Zack said, crossing his arms as he towered over him, "take your shorty pants, raggedy shoes, and your pathetic basketball skills, get on the bus, and don't butt your nose in where it doesn't belong!"

Jonah was definitely outmatched. All he could see, though, was the look on the boy's face; all he could think about was that this was wrong. Just plain wrong.

Later, Jonah would remember the next moment as simply a blur. Somehow he must have suddenly grabbed Smellman's wagging finger and used it to turn the bigger kid's arm all the way around his back.

"Hey," a surprised Snodgrass said. "Let him go!"

He and Fong moved in. Quickly, Jonah grabbed the back of Smellman's head and slammed it into the heads of both Snodgrass and Fong. He let Smellman go, and the three of them fell on the ground, in a daze. It was all over in a matter of seconds. Jonah stood over them, breathing hard as the wave of adrenaline coursed through his veins. He hadn't thought about what he was doing. Pure instinct had taken over. Then he remembered the boy again, who was still plastered against the wall.

"You okay?" he asked. The boy looked down at the three kids and then back up at Jonah, wide-eyed.

"How did you do that?" he asked. "That was awesome! You took them down, man! Wow!"

Zack and his gang were still dazed but slowly starting to stir.

"We'd better get out of here," Jonah said, quickly walking out of the alley. The boy followed him, trying to keep up, and extended his hand toward Jonah.

"I'm Freddie Johnson," he said, still smiling excitedly. "Who are you?"

"Jonah," he said, shaking the boy's hand, remembering where he had seen him before. "My sister's Eliza. I think you're in her class. And we ride the same bus."

"Oh yeah!" Freddie said. "Eliza, the reeeeeeaaaalllly smart girl. She's your sister? She's kind of cute."

"I'm afraid so—Did you say *cute*?" Jonah said, and then turned to Freddie before walking to their bus. "Hey, if you don't mind, Freddie, can we keep what just happened to ourselves?"

"But you saved my life, man!" Freddie said. He saw the look on Jonah's face, though, and said, "Okay, sure. Whatever you say." Jonah nodded and began to climb on the bus, but Freddie pulled on his arm.

"Thanks, man," he said quietly. "I owe you one."

"No problem," Jonah said, flashing a shy smile. "And you don't owe me anything."

Twice on the way home he thought he heard kids whispering. He turned around one time and saw a few kids stare at him and then quickly look away. Had Freddie said something already? He hoped not, but then again, what was the big deal if he did? He couldn't help but smile, thinking about the story spreading of how he took down Zack and his gang all by himself. He pretended to adjust the sleeve of his jacket and squeezed his own bicep. It felt the same as always. But somehow he was suddenly strong, and fast. His powers were real.

Just as he hopped off the bus and was watching Jeremiah running home ahead of him like he always did, he felt a hand grab his arm and yank him away from the group of kids.

"What happened back there?" Eliza asked.

He mustered his most innocent voice. "Uh, what do you mean?"

She pushed her glasses up her nose and frowned. "Everybody was talking about it on the bus. Whatever it was you did."

He couldn't help but smile, just a little. So it was true. Everyone *was* talking about him. Cool.

"Well?" she said, staring at him. "Are you going to say anything?"

"I don't know, Eliza," he said, starting to walk toward their house. "It all happened so fast. Zack Smellman and his buddies had Freddie pinned against the wall in the alley and they were going to beat him up. I . . ." He paused, trying to slow down the memory in his head.

"You what?"

"Well, I grabbed Zack, knocked the other two down, and they all ended up on the ground. I guess I saved Freddie from getting beaten up," Jonah said. "That was pretty much it."

She tilted her head to the side, the same move their mom made whenever she was really heated. "*Pretty much it?* I'm surprised it wasn't you they were trying to beat up today, as much as Zack hates you! And now you're telling me that you took on the three biggest bullies in the school and took care of them, just like that?"

"Apparently," Jonah said, not even trying to hide the look of satisfaction on his face now.

"Well," Eliza said, at a loss for words. "Well . . ."

"Yes, *sister*?" Jonah said, putting his arm around her, staring deeply into her eyes, mocking seriousness. She rolled her eyes.

"Look," he said, "I know that you like to worry and I appreciate you looking out for me. I do. But things are . . . changing. You'll see." He wanted so badly to tell her what happened yesterday. But he wasn't ready to. Not yet.

She shrugged his arm off of her shoulder and started to walk toward their house ahead of him. "You're going to get in trouble, Jonah. You know that, don't you? Don't you think those guys are going to go straight to the principal?"

Jonah's smile faded slightly. "What are they going to say, Eliza? Tell him that a little kid half their size took all three of them out back and whipped them? I don't think so."

Everyone is talking about what happened. He savored those words as he walked home.

∾

Jonah studied his mom carefully as she served dinner that night. She seemed so . . . normal. There was so much he wanted to ask her, but he didn't want to get into it with Eliza and Jeremiah. What were her powers? What could she do? Did she have the same amount of strength that he did, or more? Could she fly? Since she was half angel, did she have wings? Did they just sprout out of her shoulder blades when she needed them?

He watched her whip back and forth around the kitchen, pouring tall glasses of milk, fixing plates. He had never noticed it before, but she was moving fast, almost in a blur. He had never thought this was out of the ordinary—at least, not before yesterday. Now, though . . .

She glanced up at him and smiled. *Maybe she can read minds too,* he suddenly thought.

Mom, can you hear me? He concentrated really hard, squinting and trying to push the thought in her direction. *Mom, are you listening? Can you hear what I'm thinking?*

"Jonah, what are you doing?" said Jeremiah, giggling. "Your

eyes are all scrunched up on your face!" And he started copying Jonah, which made Eliza burst out laughing and his dad chuckle.

"Nothing!" Jonah said quickly, looking away from his mom. "There was just . . . something in my eye."

"The spaghetti's delicious, dear," Benjamin said. Eleanor smiled, leaning over to give him a kiss, which made Jonah roll his eyes and Jeremiah hold his nose.

"Gross!" Eliza said, frowning. "Not at the table, Mom and Dad! It's embarrassing."

Benjamin grinned at Eleanor, ignoring her comment. "How was school for everyone today?"

"Great!" Jeremiah said, in between huge bites of meatball.

Eliza's eyes sparkled, and a devious smile curved on her lips. "Why don't you ask Jonah? I heard he had a very eventful day today."

Benjamin raised his eyebrow toward his oldest son as he served himself another helping of noodles.

Jonah glared at his sister. *If only Eliza could read my mind right now . . .*

"What happened today, Jonah?" his mom asked as she sat down, tousling his hair.

"Well, math class was okay; we have a lot of homework. I had a vocabulary test today, but it was easy," he said carefully. "And, oh yeah, I almost forgot. After school there was this thing that happened with Zack and some guys, it was no big deal."

Eleanor sat up straighter. "Did they bother you, son? Were they picking on you again?"

He wanted so badly to tell them how he rescued Freddie and laid the bullies out on the ground. But he knew his mom, and he knew it would only lead to her making a phone call to

Zack's mom, or worse, coming down to the school to talk to the principal.

"Like I said, it was no big deal." He tried to smile, gulping down his last bite of spaghetti at the same time. He wanted to change the subject. "Isn't it my turn to take out the trash?"

Without waiting for an answer, he hopped up from the table.

"Jonah!" his mother said. "Plate, please!"

"Sorry, Mom," he said, spinning around and snagging his dish. He put it in the sink, grabbed the full garbage bag, and bolted out the door.

FIVE

IN THE SHADOWS

Jonah carried the garbage bag outside, glad to escape any more conversation about his run-in earlier today. He might tell his dad later, when they were alone. But when his mom felt like her kids were threatened, she could get crazy. Which was the last thing he needed at school right now.

He trudged around the corner of the house. The shadows had grown long and were about to fade away into night. Everything was that grayish color that happens just after sunset.

He smelled it before he saw it. A pungent odor that was similar to the smell of rotting garbage, only *much* stronger.

Jonah grabbed his nose. *What is that smell?*

His eyes caught movement. There was something creeping along the side of the house, just behind the plastic garbage cans. In spite of the odor, he breathed in sharply.

He could barely make out the outline of a person. Except he could tell that it wasn't exactly a *person*. It was hunched over, with what looked like two humps on its back, crusty and shriveled. As if it had been thrust into a pit of flames, then yanked out just in time. Blacker than night, it moved along the side of the house, away from him.

Jonah suddenly found it hard to breathe. He backed up and bumped against the side of the house, hitting a rake that was leaning up on the wall. It clattered to the ground.

Jonah froze, pressing himself against the wall, hoping he could somehow make himself blend into the bricks. His heartbeat was as loud as a drum in his ears.

The creature whipped around toward the noise. Its body was scaly and hard, as if it were covered by some cold, steel armor. Its face was twisted and angry. Sharp teeth protruded from its mouth. But its eyes were the scariest part.

Yellow eyes.

Yellow, and filled with hate.

Jonah felt glued to the pavement as he sensed the dark creature probe the depths of his soul with one glance. Their eyes locked onto each other's, neither of them looking away—Jonah in total fear, the creature with pure hatred.

Suddenly, before Jonah's eyes, the creature turned into a dusty black cloud, like a swarm of gnats.

And then it slowly began to move toward him.

It's coming at me! What is this thing?

Jonah didn't want to wait to find out. He pushed himself off the wall and began to run. He didn't have time to think of what to do next, or where to go. It didn't matter. He just had to get away from here.

His mountain bike was leaned up against the basketball goal in the driveway. Without looking back, he grabbed the bike, ran with it for a few steps, and then jumped on.

Frantically, Jonah began to pedal. Turning left out of his driveway, he pressed down as hard as he could, not daring to look behind him. The bike shot forward along the neighborhood street. He passed by Mr. Johnson a few houses down, just getting home from work, but he was too focused on the road to notice him wave.

Jonah felt it pursuing him. Whatever *it* was. He took rights and lefts through the tree-lined streets, and still he felt its dark presence. He pedaled faster.

Glancing down at his feet, he saw a blur of motion. A car was moving down the road ahead of him, but he realized he was gaining on it. Soon he was up on its bumper. He swung the bike around and zoomed by, not seeing the kid in the backseat pointing at him excitedly.

He'd never gone this fast before. The wind pressed against his face, and he knew that if his bike had wings, he'd be airborne by now. His angel powers were kicking in again, and he held on to the handlebars as tightly as he could.

And still, he felt the creature behind him. Gaining ground. He looked back. It was picking up speed as fast as he was.

Jonah willed his legs to move even faster. He tried to ignore the growing wobble in the tires. Every few seconds he looked over his shoulder, but as dusk deepened, he couldn't see anything.

He found himself on a long stretch of road scattered with mostly run-down, older homes. He zoomed by a few rusting trailers as he began to head down a hill. In the absence of streetlights, he was in almost complete darkness.

Jonah's breathing was heavy, and he knew he couldn't keep up this pace much longer. He felt an icy touch on his shoulder, like frozen fingers scraping his skin. Whatever was chasing him was still there. He pulled his shoulder away and ducked his head.

Just then, ahead in the distance, Jonah saw a figure, waving at him.

"Jonah!" a voice called out. "Slow down, dear."

As soon as he heard the voice, which sounded like it was coming from right beside his ear, he felt whatever it was behind him vanish. He looked back again and saw nothing but a few twinkling stars in the night sky.

He slammed on his brakes, leaving a long, black mark on the pavement.

An old woman stood in front of him, smiling kindly. She was leaning against a shovel and wearing gardening gloves and a wide-brimmed hat. Her face held deep wrinkles, but her kind, blue eyes sparkled behind her large glasses.

Jonah took in deep gasps of air, trying to catch his breath. "Hi, Mrs. Aldridge," he said, with much effort. "I didn't realize I was on your street."

Camilla Aldridge was the oldest woman in his dad's church, All Souls United Methodist. Not everyone in the congregation seemed to enjoy her company, but his parents were especially fond of her for some reason. His dad always said she was the wisest person he knew. She lived by herself in a small cottage with a beautiful garden.

"I didn't think you were going to see me, pedaling as fast as you were," she said, smiling at him. "I was just out here tidying up the garden. Always have to watch out for weeds, you know. You never know when you might spot one."

Jonah mumbled something and nodded, but his eyes darted around as she spoke.

She eyed him. "What's the matter, Jonah dear? You look like you've seen a ghost." She laughed softly and pulled off her gloves.

"Well, I guess I'm done for the evening out here. How about coming inside for a Coke before you go home?"

Under normal circumstances, Jonah would have politely said no. Hanging out with ninety-year-old women was not his idea of a good time. But there was nothing he wanted more right now than to be inside, somewhere safe, and her house seemed as good as any.

"That sounds great, Mrs. Aldridge," he said quickly. "I mean . . . uh . . . if it's not too much trouble for you."

"No, child, not at all." He followed her as she shuffled slowly down her driveway, turning around every few seconds to scan the sky.

She placed a glass full of the ice-cold soft drink in front of him on the table and began to fix herself some tea. She hummed a song as she moved around the kitchen.

Jonah's mind swirled as he finally had a chance to catch his breath. *What was that thing? Why was it sneaking around my house?* He shivered violently.

"Cold, Jonah?"

She eyed him as she placed her tea bag in the steaming mug and joined him at the table.

"Just a chill, I guess," he said uncertainly. Mrs. Aldridge was an elder in his father's church, very wise in the ways of Elohim. Even so, what would she think if he told her what he had just seen?

"Ah, just a chill?" she said as she took a sip. Her eyes searched him. "These old eyes play tricks on me sometimes, Jonah, but it seemed to me you were pedaling awfully fast down my street. Almost like you were running away from something."

"Well . . ." He tried to think. If he said out loud what was going through his mind, she was going to think he had lost it. If he told her what he had seen. . . . He shivered again, thinking about the black figure with those yellow eyes. She waited patiently for him to respond, slowly sipping her tea. He swallowed. "I . . . thought I . . . saw something. In the shadows at our house. It was probably nothing."

He tried to laugh, but it came out like a weak moan.

"Your eyes playing tricks on you too, hm?" she joked, but her smile faded just slightly, and she took another long sip of tea. "Sometimes our human eyes do deceive us, Jonah. A shadow can easily become a monster to a young, creative mind like yours. I've found that it is more important to develop your spiritual eyesight."

Jonah cocked his head, not sure he followed. "Spiritual eyesight?"

Mrs. Aldridge leaned forward and rested her elbows on the table. "For followers of Elohim, we must develop our inner vision, the ability to see into the spiritual realm. To hear what Elohim is saying. To be sensitive to the movements of His Spirit."

She said it like it was as easy as breathing, but this was all new for Jonah. He thought about the last day's events and nodded slowly. "I think I am starting to understand what you mean."

"Close your eyes," she said. He blinked at her for a minute, and then did as she said. "Now, when you were pedaling so fast down that hill just a few short minutes ago, think back. Not to what you were seeing with your eyes. What were you *sensing*? What were you *feeling* in your heart?"

Suddenly, the black creature swooped through his mind, yellow eyes glaring at him. He popped his startled eyes open.

"I was being chased," he blurted out. "By a black thing with . . . yellow eyes! It felt like being chased by . . . *hate*."

She swirled her tea bag around, staring into her mug in silence.

What she was feeling—surprise, concern, something else—he couldn't tell. But her silence bothered him. For some reason he found himself wanting to tell her about his conversation with his parents, and about his new abilities.

"Mrs. Aldridge," he finally said, "do you think what I saw was real? Or am I going crazy? Seeing things, feeling things that aren't there?"

"I think," she said, glancing at the clock on the wall, "that it's time to get you home. Your parents are bound to be wondering where you are."

"But—"

"And no," she continued, "I don't think you're crazy. Keep your eyes open, Jonah. There's another world out there. Frightening, beautiful. *And dangerous.*"

With that, she stood up and offered to drive Jonah home. And suddenly, all she wanted to talk about in the car was the best type of soil needed to grow rosebushes and how much sunlight an orchid plant needed.

Jonah sat beside her, nodding politely as he watched the darkened neighborhood streets carefully.

SIX

HENRY

The next day, Jonah went for a walk after he got home from school. He wanted to try out his powers a little more and he didn't want Eliza or Jeremiah snooping. Once he got far enough out into the woods behind his house, he practiced lifting fallen branches, some of them triple his size. After a while, he ran out of things to pick up, but the path was a lot clearer. As he moved the last few branches off to the side, he saw a flash of silver light out of the corner of his eye. But when he turned around there was nothing there.

It must have been a trick of the light, he thought, but he could have sworn—

There it was again. A flash of light, a blur of silver energy, zoomed from a perch high up in the trees down to the ground, behind some bushes.

He stared at the clump of bushes in the distance for another minute, but saw no more movement, no more blurs of light.

He approached cautiously. He knew he had seen something,

and from the way things had been going lately, it could have been anything.

Suddenly, a figure came out from behind the bushes and onto the path.

"He-hello?" Jonah said, stepping backward as the image of the black creature flashed across his mind. He prepared to run again, but the form remained motionless, like a statue in the middle of the trail.

"How long have you been able to see me?"

The voice that asked the question sounded like it was coming from a teenage boy. Jonah took a few steps closer, and the figure came into full view.

The boy looked like a regular teenager, in every way except one. He was lanky, but looked strong, and was wearing a white T-shirt and faded blue jeans. Dark, closely cropped hair matched his deep brown eyes. But behind the boy, above his head and across his shoulders, attached to his back, was a set of sparkling silver wings. The wind blew softly through the trees, and the wings fluttered, glistening, glorious, looking metallic and razor-sharp along the edges, and somehow at the same time feather-soft.

The boy glanced over his shoulder at them, then smiled at him. "What do you think about my wings, Jonah?"

Jonah blinked, moving a step closer. His mind was racing. The blur of light he had seen in the forest. Silver wings glinting in the sunlight. It was him.

"You're an . . . an . . ."

"I'm an angel," the boy said, matter-of-factly, like a kid might say, *I'm an American,* or *I'm a Miami Heat fan.*

"And that was you just now, in the trees?" Jonah asked. *So I'm not going crazy.*

"Yep, that was me," the angel said. "Was that the first time you've seen me?"

Jonah nodded as he stared. "I think so."

"Well," said the boy-angel, shoving his hands in his pockets, "it was bound to happen sometime. I mean, after Elohim revealed to you who you really are, I wondered if you'd start to see me soon. You surprised me back there, though."

Jonah was standing face-to-face with an angel. Three days ago he was not even sure that they existed. Now, not only was he staring at one, he practically *was* one. Questions began to flood Jonah's mind. "You're saying that somehow with my new . . . abilities, that I can see . . . angels?"

"Well, obviously," the boy-angel said, spreading his arms wide. "You can see me, at least."

He immediately thought of the creature he had seen, and run from, yesterday.

"Are there others like you?" Jonah asked.

The angel chuckled. "Well, of course there are, Jonah. Millions of them," he said, and then extended his hand. "Call me Henry."

Jonah looked at his hand. It looked real enough. Slowly he took it in his own. It felt like real skin, and he shook it.

"Henry, huh?" Jonah said. "An angel named Henry?"

Henry smiled. "Well, actually, Henry is a shorter version of my real name."

"Oh," Jonah replied, "okay." He paused again as he tried to get his mouth to catch up to his quickly spinning brain. "So are you my . . . guardian angel, or something?"

"I have been with you since the beginning of your life," replied Henry. "Every human family has a protector, or guardian, angel. An angel who is there to help accomplish the will of Elohim in their lives. We exist to serve Elohim and Him alone, and He assigns angels like me to be with His most prized creations." He smiled. "You."

"Am I the only one who can see you?" Jonah asked.

"This is a very rare situation, Jonah," Henry said, stroking his chin. "Very rare. For one thing, you are unique, your mom being a nephilim, as you now know. But then, to be able to see an angel without the angel choosing to reveal himself. . . . It's quite unexpected, I must admit. Elohim is up to something with you; that's for sure."

"So you are surprised that I can see you?" Jonah asked. "Excuse me for asking, but if you're an angel, aren't you and Elohim kind of on the same page? Don't you know His plans?"

Henry threw his head back and laughed. "I'm just a guardian angel. And His plans are often mysterious. Even to some angels."

Jonah struggled to collect his thoughts.

"Letting people—you know, regular humans—see you . . . this is something you can do?"

"Of course," Henry said. "But we can do a pretty good job of masking our wings and looking like real humans if we want to. Watch this."

He closed his eyes and moved his arms away from his body for a moment, and suddenly his wings became transparent.

"Cool," Jonah said, in awe. If he looked really hard, he could see the outline of Henry's wings, but he could see right through them. If he were standing farther away, or if he were not focusing on looking for them, he would have no idea they were there.

"So, yes, we can let people see us. Sometimes Elohim has an assignment for one of us that requires face-to-face interaction with a human."

"Have you ever been caught?" asked Jonah. "You know, by a human, when you were pretending to be one of us?"

"I've never been given that kind of assignment, Jonah." Henry laughed. "That's for angels much higher up in the ranks than I am. There are those who have been highly trained in such matters." He sighed, then smiled again. "But not me. I am content to be invisible, by your family's side. But to your question, there are believers who have a deep connection with Elohim, some who have a knack for spotting us."

Jonah had heard people in church occasionally talk about feeling the presence of God strongly in certain situations. The Dominguez family swore that they had been helped by an angel when their car flipped upside down last summer.

"How old are you?" Jonah asked. "I mean, you look like you're a teenager . . . except for the wings, of course."

Henry grabbed a handful of dirt in his hands and held it up. "Let's put it this way, Jonah. I was around long before this was." He let the pile of dirt sift through his slender fingers to the ground.

"You mean you're older than the planet? But you look like you're not even old enough to drive," said Jonah.

"Elohim created us," Henry said, "just as He creates all living things. Like He created you. The difference is that we don't die, so our appearance doesn't age."

"So do all of you look like teenagers?"

"Elohim is quite creative, Jonah. Just like you humans, there are no two of us who are alike."

"So," Jonah said slowly, "you've been with me . . . like, *with* me, my whole life? You've seen everything?" He gulped as he said this. There were some things in his life that he hoped no one would ever see. The thought that an angel had been invisibly following him around was unsettling.

"I'm not always right beside you, if that's what you mean," Henry said. "You get the same level of privacy from me that you would get from, say, your mom and dad. Speaking of which, I do have the rest of your family to watch over too. But let's just say that I'm close by in case you need me. I hang around."

That relieved Jonah a little. "So you were there for, say, my fifth birthday party?"

Henry grinned. "When you went to Chuck E. Cheese's and were afraid of the giant mouse? Yep, I was there." Jonah turned red, instantly wishing he hadn't brought that up. "And all of your rec league basketball games, days at school, playing video games, going on vacations. I've been right there."

That is so weird, Jonah thought. "Are there others here, then? Other angels I just can't see right now?"

Henry shrugged. "There are others around your neighborhood, your school, everywhere. Eventually you may be able to see them too. Look, Jonah, I am sure it's uncomfortable to think about invisible angels involved in your day-to-day life."

"That's the understatement of the year," Jonah mumbled.

"Just think of it like Elohim's hand working in your life," countered Henry. "It should make you feel good knowing that He cares about you so much that He sent His messengers, His hands, to guard and guide you. Pretty cool, huh?"

Jonah had to admit that this *was* pretty cool. The hands of Elohim. Angels. He had never thought of it like that, but realizing Henry had been close by all of his life made him think that maybe Elohim Himself was closer than he imagined.

"So," Jonah said, looking up from his shoes and into the eyes of his new angel-friend, "what can you do?"

Henry stared blankly. "What do you mean?"

"You know, what can you do? Like, what kind of cool stuff can you do? Flying, of course. What else?"

"Well, there are lots of different types of angels. Some who are assigned to people, like me. Others who are purely messengers, like Gabriel. Then there are those specifically created for battle. I'm sure you know who leads our army," Henry explained.

Jonah thought hard for a minute and then snapped his fingers. "Michael!"

Henry closed his eyes and nodded solemnly.

"I can do some things you humans would consider quite extraordinary," he said. "But I don't dare do anything just to show off."

"Aw, come on, Henry!" Jonah chided him. "Just show me a few tricks. I'm part angel, you know. You could consider it . . . tutoring."

Henry looked at Jonah suspiciously. "Tutoring, huh?"

Jonah nodded eagerly, and Henry rolled his eyes, but Jonah had a feeling that he wouldn't have to twist his arm too hard to get him to do something.

"Please?" Jonah begged. "How else will I learn? I could hurt myself, you know, or someone in my family, if I don't learn to control these powers."

That was all it took. Henry straightened his back, flapped his wings, and began to rise slowly off the ground. Then he sprang upward, so fast that Jonah had a hard time following him. He shot straight up, directly overhead, until all Jonah could see was a glittering speck that eventually disappeared into a white, fluffy cloud. Jonah stared at the cloud for half a minute but saw nothing. He began to wonder if he had annoyed Henry after all. Then suddenly, a gleam of silver burst through the cloud and was coming right at him, fast as a missile fired from a jet. But just over the tops of the trees, Henry slowed down, until he was floating down to the ground like a graceful feather, with his arms folded, right in front of Jonah.

"Whoa," Jonah said, impressed. "That was amazing!"

"It's no big deal. Something I do every day," Henry said, suppressing a grin. "Now listen, Jonah, I think it's about time you headed home."

"Just one more thing, Henry," Jonah pleaded. "Just show me one more power."

Henry sighed, but held up a single index finger and said, "One more."

He stepped out from the trees and into the Stones' backyard, turning toward the small pond. Reaching back over his shoulder, out of nowhere, he pulled a flaming arrow, at the same time that a bow suddenly appeared in his left hand. He strung the arrow and aimed it at the sky, pulling back and letting it fly.

The arrow shot out of his hands, and Jonah and Henry watched the flaming arc burn across the darkening sky. It finally turned back toward the earth, falling, falling, until it dropped with a fizzle and *splash* into the middle of the pond.

"Okay, you *have* to show me how to do that," Jonah exclaimed.

Henry watched the water ripples move outward to the edges of the pond as he spoke. "Angels have a closely connected relationship with Elohim, Jonah. It's a connection we are born with. One that human beings do not naturally have. It can be attained, of course, but it is difficult. That's where my ability comes from. You may be able to develop these kinds of powers, being a quarterling, but it will all be in Elohim's timing. Just like finding your super-strength." He eyed Jonah now. "And one thing to always remember, Jonah. Your true power will come through dependence and trust, not force and will."

Jonah heard his mother's voice calling from the house, "Jonah! Time for dinner!"

"Sounds like it's time to go," Henry said.

He reluctantly agreed, and they turned to walk toward the house.

"Keep your eyes open, Jonah," Henry said when they were almost to the door. "There are other creatures you may begin to see. Dangerous ones. Like us, but . . . well, also very different. They can inhabit people, or even animals, and control them. They call it 'Holding.'"

Jonah remembered the icy touch of the creature that had chased him the night before, and shivered. He was about to ask Henry about the incident, but his mom called him again. He ate his dinner quietly, unable to get Henry's last warning out of his thoughts.

SEVEN

THE TAKING

It was Wednesday morning, which meant housecleaning day around the Stone home. If she didn't put it on the schedule, it would never get done. So every week, on the same day, Eleanor vacuumed, mopped, and otherwise straightened up.

Not that it took her very long. When there was no one else home, she didn't mind putting some of her nephilim abilities to good use. She sped around the house in a blur, and in no time, she had it looking great. Plus, it wasn't a bad workout.

She looked at the clock. Just enough time to shower and change, then meet a couple of friends for lunch before the kids came home from school.

She was about to head upstairs when the doorbell rang.

Glancing out the window on her way to the door, she noticed a white van, which had "Action Cable Television" emblazoned across its windowless sides, backed into their driveway underneath the basketball hoop. Action Cable was the largest provider of cable service in the state of New Jersey, and the company of choice in their neighborhood.

Eleanor opened the door to two people wearing navy jackets that bore the cable company's red, white, and blue logo. A stocky, bald man with a poorly fitting company hat stood on her left. There was some kind of tattoo across his neck and up across the back of his scalp. He was trying to manage a smile, but it came out more like someone had stepped on his toe.

A thin woman with sunken cheeks stood to the right, her hat pulled low. She was staring at Eleanor's feet.

"Good morning," Eleanor said, pushing a strand of hair out of her face. "I didn't realize we were having problems with our television. Did my husband call you?"

But even as the words left her lips, she locked eyes with the bald man, and in an instant, somehow, she knew exactly who they were. Her own eyes grew wide, suddenly full of terror.

It was the color of his eyes, burning yellow.

Before Eleanor could turn, or fight, or even scream, the bald man moved quickly inside the door. His hand closed like a vise around the back of her neck, and he covered her mouth with a black cloth he had pulled from his pocket. It muffled her scream, and he held her there tightly. The woman grabbed her, and together they wrestled her down inside the doorway, waiting for the ten seconds it would take for the chemical in the cloth to do its job.

Finally, her eyes closed and she grew limp on the floor.

The woman was already scanning the streets outside.

"It looks clear, Marduk," she said.

"What did I say to you about using my real name, Dionyss?" He glared at her, his voice dripping with disgust.

Dionyss looked down at the carpet, bowing her head. "I'm sorry, Commander. Forgive me."

Marduk grunted and waved her off, pushing his head with his hand until his neck popped loudly. He rubbed the back of his skull, along the tattoo of a large, black handprint. He was still trying to get used to his latest body. It had been a while since he had occupied someone. His role had always been to lord over his band of fallen ones in the Second Region: to rule them, to organize them, and send them to do his master's bidding. His objective was to influence those in influential positions, to turn a thought in the right direction, to whisper in a willing ear, to monitor the progress of the war—and to report to his master, of course.

But sometimes a good Holding was what the job demanded. It had taken over three years of patient work for this plan to unfold, and now was one of those times.

Dionyss had occupied her host's body for almost that entire time. She had watched the Stone house every day for the past several months. Long enough to know that the three kids would be at school and the husband would be at the church. No company. No neighbors going to and fro. Their timing was perfect.

Marduk put the cloth back into a plastic bag and stuffed it in his pocket. He was pleased. Kidnapping a nephilim was serious, even for someone like him. He had come prepared for resistance. He'd only dealt with nephilim a handful of times, the last time thousands of years ago. But he remembered. The power of these creatures was special, unique. Both human and angel, they possessed enormous capabilities. *But also one supreme weakness*, he reminded himself. Which was why they had come in the first place.

He studied Eleanor's face and then stroked her cheek lightly.

"You do look like your mother, that's for sure."

Marduk pulled thick chains out of the bag Dionyss had carried in and wrapped them tightly around Eleanor's wrists. He snapped a lock on them, while Dionyss did the same with Eleanor's feet. After taping her mouth, they fit a long, black bag over her head, pulling it all the way down to her shoes. Marduk threw her over his shoulder and, with Dionyss carefully keeping watch for any unexpected observers, they crept back outside to the back of the van. Quickly, he laid Eleanor inside and slammed the double doors shut.

They jumped into the van and sped out of the driveway, disappearing down the sunny, tree-lined street.

cಗಿ

Benjamin was in his office at church, working on next Sunday's message, when he felt an overwhelming sense that something was desperately wrong. He had felt strong urges to pray before, usually for his family or for people in the church.

But never anything like this.

The feeling all but forced him out of his chair and onto the floor beside his desk. His heart felt dark, heavy.

What is it, Elohim? What do You want me to do?

Pray, My son. The voice was strong within his heart.

He didn't have to ask for whom. The name was already on his lips.

"Eleanor . . ."

He bent his face down to the carpet and began to pray.

PART II

INTO THE CITY

*Then the dragon was very angry at the woman,
and he went off to make war against all her other
children—those who obey God's commands
and who have the message Jesus taught.*

Revelation 12:17 NCV

EIGHT

VISITORS AT THE DOOR

Benjamin came home to strangers waiting for him on his front porch.

A large man with a chiseled face, wearing a black suit, stood beside a striking woman with red hair, also dressed in black. Their eyes were bright and strangely comforting, and he found himself drawn in.

"Are you two . . . selling something?" Benjamin asked weakly, even though in his heart he knew the answer was no.

"Can we come in, Benjamin?" the man said, ignoring the question.

Benjamin hesitated, but continued to stare at them, saying nothing.

The woman stepped forward. "It's about your wife. It's about Eleanor."

They knew something about her. He snapped back to life. "What about her? Where is she?"

She studied him for a few seconds. "She's been taken."

Jonah strolled home from the bus stop that sunny afternoon, eager for a snack and to catch up with his friend Tariq. They had spent the summer working on a fort in the woods that they called "Project X," and it was almost finished. Eliza walked behind him with a couple of friends, and then plopped down on the curb, going over the results of their latest math test. Jeremiah had taken a different bus home with a boy from school.

He bounded through the door and threw his book bag in the corner, making a beeline for the refrigerator.

"Mom, I'm home!" he called out, opening the fridge door and searching for a snack. He looked around to make sure no one was watching, and then reached down for the half gallon of orange juice, popping the top off and chugging a few gulps, straight from the carton.

"Son . . ."

He quickly put the juice container down and wiped his face. He hadn't even noticed his dad, who had just stood up from the sofa in the den.

"Dad? What are you doing home so—?"

Two people, a man and a woman in business suits, stood up behind Benjamin. The man looked like his muscles were about to explode through his jacket. The woman had fiery red hair and an intense gaze.

Henry, the Stone family's guardian angel, stepped around to the side of the huge man. The man nodded at him and Jonah realized he could see Henry. That was weird.

"Jonah," his dad stammered, like he wasn't sure what he

wanted to say. "These people are . . . well, they're here to help with . . . they are investigators." He was trying to compose himself, but wasn't doing a great job of it. His eyes welled up with tears, even though he tried to hold them back.

"Investigators?" Jonah repeated. "Like . . . police? Dad, what's wrong?"

Benjamin glanced at the woman, who nodded. He sighed loudly, pulling the glasses off his face. "Mom's been taken. Someone kidnapped her."

Jonah froze, trying to understand the words his father had just said.

"What do you mean, kidnapped?" he said, and then crossed his arms. "How do you know?"

The man in the suit cleared his throat. "Our best intelligence suggests that she was taken a few hours ago."

Jonah shook his head. "She's probably just out. Maybe for a run, or at the store or something. Right, Dad?" He looked at Benjamin, hoping he would agree. Instead, his father looked away.

Jonah stared at the two strangers. "Who are you? Are you really police? Where's your patrol car? If it's true, shouldn't there be a dozen cops scouring this place by now? Where are they?" He squinted at them and then looked at Henry. If they could see Henry, then they definitely weren't cops. "You aren't police, are you?"

The woman looked up at her partner. "We might as well let him see who we are. After all, we are here to talk to him too."

Suddenly, they began to transform. The suits faded away. In place of them, armor appeared across their torsos and legs. It was black and silver and looked like steel, covering most of their bodies.

Silvery wings sprouted from their shoulders, and the ones on the man looked like they'd engulf the entire room if he spread them out fully. On his left wrist he wore a silver band that looked like a regular wristwatch.

The female angel was smaller but just as impressive. Her hair was sunset orange, streaked with yellow and white. And her eyes blazed with fire.

Jonah shivered as he studied their faces. They were strong, fierce, but somehow kind, all at once. These were angels of war. Jonah would bet anything that they served under the archangel and battle-warrior Michael's command. Henry had his wings on display too, but was still wearing jeans and a white T-shirt.

"Um . . ." Jonah couldn't find the right words. "You're . . . you're . . ."

"Angels," the female one said, smiling slightly. "I'm Taryn. And this is Marcus. It's nice to meet you, Jonah."

Jonah's mouth hung open.

"I came home just a little while ago. I felt in my heart that something had happened to your mother," Benjamin said, calmly at first, but his voice grew more and more strained as he went on. "Marcus and Taryn were waiting for me on the porch. They knew what happened—Eleanor was kidnapped. By . . . by Abaddon." He sank onto the sofa and covered his face with his hands.

Henry moved to the sofa to comfort Jonah's dad.

Marcus stood perfectly still, his arms folded across his chest. "Reverend Stone, you have done the right thing. There is no point in calling the human police. They cannot do anything to help under these circumstances. For years we have kept close tabs on Eleanor Stone, closer than you have realized. She has always been a person of . . . interest to us. As a nephilim, an exceptionally power-ful creature, we wanted to monitor her . . . safety," he said. He seemed to be picking his words carefully.

"Oh, don't beat around the bush, Marcus! I know what you think," Benjamin suddenly shot back. "I know how you all feel about the nephilim. You think they are uncontrollable, dangerous, and prone to great evil! And yet Eleanor and I have always led peaceful lives."

Jonah saw indignation burn hotly in Marcus's eyes. "Only because that is what I have seen, Reverend Stone. *With my own eyes*. They have a great weakness. They can easily be manipul—"

Jonah's father stood up. "I will not have Eleanor disrespected in her own house by you or anyone else, even if you are under Michael's authority! She is kindhearted, self-controlled, and I daresay loves Elohim as much as anyone in this room! You are referring to things that happened thousands of years ago and have nothing to do with her." He and Marcus locked eyes and said nothing, smoldering silence shaking the room.

Taryn stepped forward, her wings expanding slightly. "Both of you. That is enough," she said, eyeing Marcus. "We are here to share our intelligence with you and to assure you, Benjamin, that Elohim has a plan. Even in all of this. Our sources have indicated that her kidnappers did not kill her but are taking her somewhere. They have a purpose in mind. Which means they will keep her alive."

Marcus relaxed slightly and said, "Taryn is right. Abaddon must not want her dead."

"And at this point," Taryn continued, "that is a good thing."

"*At this point?*" Jonah asked. "What does that mean?"

Taryn looked at him for a few seconds, as if she were measuring him up somehow. "I simply mean that the best time to retrieve her is now."

Jonah couldn't believe what he was hearing. *Is this some kind of weird daydream?* No, he was really here, and there were three angels talking with his dad in the living room. *Mom's been kidnapped.* Angry tears began to form in his eyes. *Abaddon and his fallen ones took my mother.*

Taryn glanced at Marcus quickly before she spoke again. "There's something else. Our sources tell us that there were apparently others who were taken today as well."

"Others?" Jonah's dad said, confused. "You mean, other . . . ?"

"Nephilim," she said. "We have been monitoring not only Eleanor but others as well. Across the world."

"How many others?"

"Seven," said Taryn. "Eleanor makes eight."

Benjamin sighed. "I thought she was the only one." He had taken his seat back on the sofa. "What does this mean?"

"It is quite possible that there is a larger plan at work here. That the fallen ones are up to something . . . big. These are certainly more than just random kidnappings," Taryn answered.

"Why would the Fallen want to kidnap eight nephilim at the same time?" Jonah asked.

Silence.

"If you must know," Marcus finally said, "we believe this was his plan from the beginning. That he intended to do this all along."

"All along?" Jonah's father repeated, looking confused.

"Yes," Marcus said quietly. "Ever since he planted them here."

The room was silent again, until finally Benjamin spoke quietly. "You said . . . *planted*?"

Marcus nodded.

"You mean to tell me that the nephilim, their existence on earth . . . my wife's existence . . . has all been part of some *plan*

Abaddon has?" The disbelief was clear now in Benjamin's voice. "That Abaddon sent his own fallen angels to find human women and have children through them? You can't be serious!"

Taryn spoke up. "It is not that far-fetched, Reverend Stone. We are confident that this is part of his plan, which has yet to unfold fully. We intend to make sure that it never does." Her confidence helped Jonah breathe a little slower. She spoke more softly now. "And by the way, of course we do not wish to imply that Eleanor Stone is an evil person. Clearly, Elohim has done much through and around her."

"But you said yourself," replied Benjamin, brushing off the compliment, "that the nephilim have a capacity for great evil in our world. Exactly what kind of evil are you talking about?"

Marcus moved to the window, his back toward Benjamin. "Do you know why Elohim flooded this world?"

"Because of the sin of mankind," Benjamin answered. "It had grown so atrocious that He brought an end to the world. Only Noah and his family survived."

"Yes," Marcus said. "Dark days in the kingdom. Very dark. But, Reverend Stone, do you know who the ringleaders of human wickedness were in those days before the flood?"

Benjamin was quiet.

"Nephilim," Marcus said, unable to hide the disgust in his voice. "They were there, leading mankind astray. Influencing them. Using their abilities to incite great violence and sin in men and women, against each other. *Against Elohim.*"

Benjamin rose up from the sofa again.

"My Eleanor is not like that!" he yelled, approaching Marcus. "She is not like they were! You don't know anything about her!"

"What *you* don't know is that some of the greatest, most-feared warriors and leaders this world has ever known were nephilim," the angel said, glaring at him. "Attila the Hun. Genghis Khan. Joseph Stalin."

Benjamin's mouth dropped. "All of them were . . . ?"

Marcus nodded. "Imagine eight Genghis Khans united under Abaddon's thumb."

Taryn stepped in between them now.

"We pray that you are right about Eleanor, Benjamin," she said, her hand against his chest. "But for now, let's just focus on the task at hand. Time is running short."

Benjamin backed off, his eyes drifting to the window. "Just one more question," he said quietly. "What does Elohim have to say about all of this?"

Jonah had been wondering the same thing.

"As you know, Reverend, He is personal, and yet mysterious. Even to angels." Marcus offered a hint of a smile for the first time. "But one thing you can always be sure of: He sees, He knows, and He is watching. There is nothing that surprises Him. And He will speak, and act, when He deems it necessary. We have our orders from Him. That is enough."

"So what exactly are we going to do?" Jonah asked.

Benjamin turned around to face Marcus, Taryn, and Henry. "I'm going to get her back." He stared defiantly at Marcus, waiting for him to respond.

"No, you aren't," Marcus said quietly, locking his eyes with Benjamin, then glancing past him to Jonah. "And neither are we."

Benjamin's eyes narrowed and his forehead wrinkled.

"What exactly is that supposed to mean? We can't just leave her to Abaddon!"

"That task has been assigned to Jonah and Eliza," Taryn said evenly. "We are simply here to deliver the orders."

Benjamin moved between the angels and Jonah.

"Im-impossible!" he stammered. "I won't allow it! Are you two insane? Do you know what you are saying? You want to send two children out against the Fallen? Against Abaddon himself?"

"We understand how you must feel," said Taryn. "And I know this will be a difficult test for you as well. But our orders—"

"Our orders are clear," Marcus interrupted, "as hard as they may be to hear. The mission is theirs, and theirs alone. They may be children, but angel blood courses through their veins. It is the will of Elohim."

Benjamin started to speak again, but suddenly it seemed as though the fight had gone out of him. *It is the will of Elohim.* Jonah knew how much those words must weigh for his father. Benjamin leaned over, snatched his glasses off his face, and put both hands on his knees.

"Eliza too?" he finally whispered. "She doesn't even know who she is yet . . ."

Taryn moved closer to him, compassion in her eyes. "It is time that she knew."

Jonah's mind was spinning. How were they supposed to rescue their mother from the forces of darkness? They were just kids. But the words of the angel echoed inside his head. *It is the will of Elohim.* God was trusting him with a mission. He'd been chosen. And his mother needed his help. Jonah felt himself stand a little taller. He stepped forward and put a hand on his dad's shoulder.

"Dad . . ."

His father placed his hand on top of Jonah's, looked back up at Marcus and Taryn with tears in his eyes, and whispered, "I just can't lose Eleanor and two of my children in the same day."

"I know why you feel that way," Taryn said gently. "But they will go with the favor of Elohim. We must trust Him."

Marcus stood with his arms folded again, looking sternly at Jonah. Jonah wasn't sure, but he thought the mighty angel appeared less than excited about this too.

"So how does this work?" Jonah finally said. "I mean, how are we supposed to find her?"

Marcus took the thing that looked like a watch off of his wrist.

"You'll need this," he said, snapping it around Jonah's arm.

"I'll need to know what time it is?" Jonah asked, looking at the silver band with the large, round face. There were two fancy, scrolled hands that pointed to numbers like any other watch. Currently it read 3:57. "Um, it's a nice watch and all, but how is this supposed to help us find Mom?"

"Push the button," he said.

Jonah pressed the knob on the side. The watch hands dissolved away and the face glowed orange. It was now a digital display, with strange markings running across it. Some kind of language Jonah couldn't read.

"Sorry," Marcus said, grabbing his arm to look. "Need to change it from the Angelic tongue to English." He gave the knob a turn. It said:

Mission: Recover Eleanor Stone
Priority: Critical
Location: Manhattan Island, New York City
Further instructions upon arrival

"This is not just a watch, Jonah," said Marcus. "It's a warrior-class, military-grade angelic navigation system. This one is a MissionFinder 3000. It will give you direction when you're not sure where to go."

"MissionFinder 3000," Jonah repeated, admiring the device. He pushed the knob again, and it morphed back into the watch face. "Cool."

"A gadget like this will help you," Taryn said, "but remember, Jonah—the Spirit of Elohim is always with you. He is there to guide you on your journey."

Marcus nodded.

"Jonah." He turned to see his father, who had tears running down his cheeks. His dad grabbed him in a bear hug. "I . . . I love you, son," he finally whispered, hugging Jonah so tight he was afraid he might crack his ribs. "Your mom and I . . . we never meant . . . we never thought that anything like this could happen. But as much as I am afraid, and as much as I wish I could take your place right now, you and Eliza have to do what Elohim is telling you to do. I would never stand in the way of that. He has a plan."

"Thanks, Dad," Jonah said, feeling both worry and excitement course through his body.

"Speaking of Eliza," Benjamin said wearily, "I guess it's time to tell her too."

"Not necessary," came a shaky voice from behind them. "Are those really angels? Standing in our living room?"

They all turned to see Eliza emerge from the hallway, wide-eyed, staring at them all.

NINE

THE MESSENGER

"Y ou can see them, Eliza dear?" asked Benjamin. "The angels?"

"Of course I can." She straightened her glasses and pushed a curly wisp of hair out of her eyes. "Those are *costumes*, right?"

Marcus chuckled and expanded his wings again, filling the room with glittering silver.

"Costumes?"

Eliza gasped. "You mean, you're *real*?"

Taryn smiled, bowing her head slightly. All of the color drained from Eliza's face as she stood speechless.

Benjamin heaved a sigh, sat down on the sofa, and patted the cushion beside him. "Come sit down, dear. There are some things you need to know. Can you give us a few minutes, friends?"

Marcus spoke haltingly. "Time is of the essen—"

"Of course we can," Taryn interrupted, pulling Marcus down the hallway with her.

"You're going to find what I'm about to tell you hard to believe," Benjamin began. "But I assure you, Eliza, it is all true."

Then he started back at the beginning, the same way he had with Jonah. He told her about the battles being waged between good and evil, among the angels of Elohim and the Fallen of Abaddon, and who their mother really was—a nephilim.

"Which makes her three children—"

"Quarterlings," Jonah interrupted eagerly. "You, me, and Jeremiah—we are one-quarter angel. Which means we have a special connection with Elohim and the angels. And certain . . . powers."

Eliza smirked. "Like Superman or something? Really, Jonah?"

He shrugged his shoulders, and Benjamin nodded to him. Jonah grabbed the sofa where his father and sister were sitting and lifted it over his head like he would a tissue box.

When Jonah set them back down, he saw that Eliza's mouth was open but no sound came out.

"Each of you has gifts. Angel powers," Benjamin said, as Jonah took a seat next to him on the sofa. "Jonah seems to possess a superhuman strength. But angel gifts, like human gifts, are unique to the person. And more than one may appear."

"Zack and the bullies in the alleyway," said Eliza, nodding slowly at Jonah.

Jonah raised his eyebrows. Benjamin looked curiously at both of them but said nothing.

Eliza stood up slowly from the sofa, stooped down, and began to pull. She strained but couldn't budge it.

"Nothing to worry about, Eliza," said Benjamin. "Your gifts will present themselves when they are needed."

Marcus stepped back into the room, Taryn behind him.

"We can't waste any more time," Marcus said. "Did you tell her about the mission?"

Benjamin sighed again. "We were just getting to that, Marcus, but listen, I don't agree—"

"It's not for you to determine," Marcus said loudly and impatiently. "It is for Jonah and Eliza to decide."

Jonah spoke up. "Look, Eliza, I don't totally get it, but Marcus and Taryn are here to deliver orders—to us." He took a deep breath. "Mom's been kidnapped. And we are the ones who have to rescue her."

"She's been . . . *what*?" Eliza searched all of their faces. They each nodded silently. She swallowed hard. Her forehead creased, a visible sign of her mind working to make sense of it all.

"Who took her? Why aren't the police here?"

"Because she wasn't kidnapped by humans, Eliza," said Jonah. "She was kidnapped by fallen angels."

"That's why we're here," Taryn said, trying to ease the tension. "Let us come together, dear friends. Let us listen for Elohim." She extended her hands to Jonah and Eliza. Benjamin, Henry, and Marcus joined in, and they stood in a circle in the Stone family living room. She closed her eyes. Everyone else followed her lead.

Jonah began to feel strangely calm and focused. Strength and peace washed over him, slowly replacing the fear that had been threatening to overpower him ever since he had heard his mother had been taken. He breathed in and out, feeling cleansed with love and protection. *Is this Elohim?* His eyes remained closed. *Is He near?* It sure felt that way. He wondered if Eliza and the others felt the same thing. He cracked one eye open, and one look answered that question. The confusion on her face was gone, replaced by a peaceful glow. The same glow he saw on everyone's face in the circle.

Eliza opened her eyes and calmly said, "Okay. I'm in. So, when do we leave?"

Jonah could not go to sleep, so he stared at the ceiling. After a hushed but fierce argument between the angels and their dad, Marcus and Taryn had agreed for Jonah and Eliza to leave at first light. So reluctantly, he and Eliza had gone to bed to try to get a few hours of sleep.

Jonah closed his eyes and tried to pray, but as soon as he did, he saw his mom. They were in the kitchen together, just Jonah and her, face-to-face.

"Jonah," Eleanor whispered, sucking in air heavily as if she were out of breath. "Listen to me, Jonah. Watch out. Be careful. Keep your eyes open. Abaddon . . . he wants to . . . to . . ."

But before she could finish this sentence, her mouth began to open wide. It grew larger and larger, as though it were being forced open from the inside. Suddenly, two yellow eyes emerged from her open throat. The creature, the fallen one Jonah had seen beside the house, came out, its own mouth open, razor-sharp teeth reaching toward him. Eleanor's body fell on the ground like a wrinkled sheet. The creature struck at him quickly, like a cobra, and Jonah turned aside, throwing his arms up in front of his face, and leaned back, screaming, waiting for the pain.

He sat up straight in bed, sweating through his T-shirt, craning his neck out in front of him, looking for two yellow eyes. *It was just a dream.* The red numbers on the alarm clock read 1:33 a.m. Pulling off his covers, he hopped down from his top bunk and stumbled across the room.

He pulled on his old jeans and changed into another T-shirt, and then quietly emptied his life savings out of the tennis ball can—all $117.33 of it—stuffing it down in his pocket. He grabbed his old blue jacket and nothing else. They would need to travel light, and he hoped they wouldn't be gone for very long anyway.

He found Eliza standing in her doorway, clearly unable to sleep too.

"You ready, sis?"

She frowned. "But the angels and Dad said to wait until morning."

"I don't know about you, but I don't think I'm getting any more sleep tonight," he said matter-of-factly. "It's our mission, Eliza. And I can't just sit here knowing Mom's out there somewhere."

She pursed her lips but nodded in agreement and went back in her room to get dressed in the dark.

They bounded down the stairs as fast as they could. So fast that they almost didn't notice the knock on the front door.

Jonah screeched to a halt and looked at the door. Who would be out there at this time of night? He saw the face of an old woman peering through the small window. She smiled and waved at them both. It was Camilla Aldridge.

"Jonah! Eliza dear!" she said as he opened the door, giving them frail hugs and placing a bony hand on their cheeks. "How are you both?" Her eyes seemed to hold them in place, and even though they needed to go, they found themselves unable to turn away from her gaze.

"We're fine, Mrs. Aldridge," Jonah said in a whisper, hoping Mrs. Aldridge would catch the hint and lower her voice. "Kind of tired, I guess. Middle of the night and everything." *She must be wondering why we're up right now*, he thought. *But then again, she's up too.* "Uh, are you here to see Dad?"

She walked in and placed her purse on the chair, ignoring his question, and turned her blue eyes toward them again. Her voice started slowly, but was strong, filling up Jonah's ears, his mind, and his soul with words that sounded alive, somehow. "Listen carefully, dear ones. Ephesians 6:10–17: 'Be strong in the Lord and in the power of His might. Put on the whole armor of God, that you may be able to stand against the wiles of the devil. For we do not wrestle against flesh and blood, but against principalities, against powers, against the rulers of the darkness of this age, against spiritual hosts of wickedness in the heavenly places. Therefore take up the whole armor of God, that you may be able to withstand in the evil day, and having done all, to stand. Stand therefore, having girded your waist with truth, having put on the breastplate of righteousness, and having shod your feet with the preparation of the gospel of peace; above all, taking the shield of faith with which you will be able to quench all the fiery darts of the wicked one. And take the helmet of salvation, and the sword of the Spirit, which is the word of God.'"

She nodded at Jonah and Eliza, making sure they had heard every word she said. Then she took a small black book out of her purse, placed it in Jonah's hand, and pressed his fingers around it. He looked down and saw that it was a small Bible with a bookmark in it. She squeezed his shoulders tightly. He smiled shyly at her and, muttering a "Thanks," shoved the book in his back pocket and turned to go.

"Be blessed, dear children," she said. "Take that book wherever you go. You just may need it. And remember that scripture. Ephesians 6. Remember, young ones." She smiled, and in that split second, Jonah knew that she knew. She knew where they were going and what they were going to do. And she was not trying to stop them.

She was sending them off with a blessing.

"Okay," Jonah said. "Uh . . . thanks, Mrs. Aldridge."

They waved a quick good-bye and made a beeline for the garage. Once in the garage, they grabbed their bikes and began strapping on their helmets.

"A mission from Elohim," Eliza said, as she fiddled with her strap. "I can't believe it. Why would He trust a thirteen-year-old and an eleven-year-old with something so huge?"

Jonah snapped his black helmet on. "I don't know, Eliza. But He did. He must really believe we can do it."

She smiled at that idea, then cocked her head to the side. "One more question. Where exactly are we going?"

TEN

Encounter on the Road

"We have to get to New York," Jonah said, looking at the watch Marcus gave him, the MissionFinder 3000. He showed it to her, told her what the angel said, and watched her *ooh* and *aah* over it for a minute. "We can catch a train in Peacefield that will take us to the subway station in Newark. And then we ride the subway from Newark to New York City, just like when we go with Mom and Dad."

He had a rope from Boy Scouts in the garage and cut a piece of it off. He tied one end to Eliza's bike and the other to his.

"What's that for?" she asked, touching the rope. "Do you expect us to ride hooked together?"

"Trust me, you're going to want to stay attached to me for this ride. You haven't seen me pedal a bike lately. I'm a little bit faster than I used to be."

They walked their bikes out into the crisp night air. The sky overhead twinkled with stars, and the whole world felt empty with everyone they knew fast asleep in their beds. Jonah made sure that no one was coming down the road in either direction, and he hopped on his bicycle.

"Get on yours too," he instructed. Eliza hopped on and looked at him eagerly, waiting for his next command. "Ready?"

She nodded, gripping her handlebars tightly.

"Here we go!" Jonah began pedaling. He pulled off slowly, his bike twisting and turning, the extra weight almost pulling him down onto the pavement.

"Hey!" she yelled, trying to control her bike, which was going all over the road too.

"Hold on!" he called back. "I need a minute to get used to the extra weight."

They moved forward and began descending the hill just beyond their house. He glanced around and saw that no cars or people were coming. It was now or never. Jonah had the feel of Eliza's bike behind him, so he began to pedal. Faster and faster. He felt strong, like he could pedal all day, and looking down at his feet, all he saw was a white blur. He only dared to look back at Eliza for a second, because he didn't want to take his eyes off the road. But when he did look back, he caught a glimpse of her face, and saw a look of pure excitement.

Jonah could have gone faster, but he didn't want to get out of control. He tried to keep it on the edge of the speed he could handle. Any faster and they could end up splattered all across Cranberry Street.

He mainly tried to keep his eyes on the road ahead. Skillfully, he made a right turn, and then a left, until they were on a long stretch of empty road that would eventually lead them into the city. No more turns for a few minutes and Jonah could relax a little. He looked back to check on Eliza, when something else caught his eye. A figure had jumped out of the woods.

And whatever it was, it began to chase them.

He could tell that it wasn't a person. It ran on four powerful legs, and in the pale moonlight, he saw a flash of teeth and bright yellow eyes. Was he seeing things? He swallowed and looked harder. Whatever it was, it was still there. And gaining on them quickly.

Then another animal emerged from the woods and joined the chase.

And then a third. Another appeared, and then four more at once, tearing out of the forest, baring their sharp teeth as they sprinted toward the bikes. They looked like some kind of huge cat, and he suddenly remembered that last week his dad said that authorities had killed a rabid cougar in the woods around Peacefield. *Is that what these animals are?* His hands were now covered in sweat, and he squeezed his handlebar grips tighter to try and hold on.

"Eliza!" he said, pedaling furiously. "Look back!"

She turned her head to see the eight animals charging behind them. She turned back to Jonah, mouth hanging open, eyes wide.

He was already pedaling fast, but adrenaline was coursing through his system now, and his feet moved even faster. The old mountain bike had been his dad's before it was his, and for the first time he thought about the fact that it might not be built for this kind of speed. The handlebars were starting to vibrate. He tried to ignore them and bore down harder.

He heard the growls growing louder and knew that even though he was moving his legs as fast as he could, somehow they were getting closer.

"Go, Jonah, go!" Eliza screamed. "Faster!"

"I'm doing the best I can!" he yelled back at her. What did she think, that he could just press the accelerator a little bit harder and pull away? They weren't in a car, and it wasn't easy to go this fast.

They flew down the straight shot of highway, with nothing ahead of them except a strip of dark black pavement, woods on every side—no houses, no buildings, nowhere to stop, nowhere to hide.

Suddenly, he spotted four figures ahead of him on the road. They were pacing back and forth, blocking their way. Jonah could see their dark shapes cut across the moonlight, the flex of their muscles as they moved, and four pairs of yellow eyes glaring at them in the distance.

"Hit the brakes, Eliza! Hit the brakes!" he said, and he began squeezing his hand brakes. She did too, to Jonah's immense relief; if she hadn't, she would have gone flying past him, and the rope that still held their two bikes together would cause her to soar over her handlebars.

They screeched to a stop in the middle of the road. The eight cougars behind them slowed down, until they were only about thirty feet away. They began to pace back and forth, baring their teeth and growling. The four in front quickly joined the others in their pack until they had their prey surrounded. There would be no running into the woods, or down the road, or anywhere else.

They were trapped.

"They're definitely cougars," Eliza said, pushing her glasses up on her nose as she hopped carefully from her bike, causing it to rattle a little with her trembling. "One of the largest cats in North America, from the genus Puma. Cougars were thought to be extinct around here until recently, when . . ."

"Will you just shut up for a minute, Eliza!" Jonah snapped. *We need a solution, not a science lesson.* They stepped toward each other and stood back to back.

"Look at their eyes," Eliza said. "They look . . . strange."

"Yeah," said Jonah. "I noticed that too. They're yellow. Listen, Eliza. I saw a fallen one by our house a few days ago. Its eyes were yellow too. This is not good."

Their backs were against each other, and Eliza grabbed his hand and squeezed it tightly in hers. They stood in between their two bikes and turned slowly in a circle, Jonah's eyes darting wildly around as he tried to keep tabs on all of the beasts.

The cougars were circling around them, licking their mouths and watching them. With each passing second, they were inching their way closer, and the circle around Jonah and Eliza was growing smaller.

"Jonah," Eliza whispered, "what are we going to do?"

He heard the desperation in her voice and wished he had a good answer, something that would give her hope that there was a way out of this.

A large cougar, the biggest of the pack, had locked its eyes on Jonah. It was just inside the circle created by the other eleven, a little closer than the rest. Its yellow eyes glared at them, full of hate, if that were possible for an animal.

They both knew what was about to happen.

"Elohim, help us!" Jonah prayed, closing his eyes and shielding his face with his arms.

The cougar jumped. Eliza's scream ripped through Jonah's ears, tearing through the dark sky, and Jonah hunched down, bracing himself for the cat to land on them and start tearing into them with its teeth and claws. Instead, he heard a loud thud above him and a high-pitched squeal that sounded more like someone had kicked a house pet. There was no clawing, and no biting.

Confused, Jonah opened his eyes and looked up. Above him stood Eliza, who looked just as bewildered as he did, her hands outstretched toward the sky. From her fingertips down to the ground, all around them, like half of the moon had fallen on top of them in the middle of the street, were thin beams of light. There were thousands of them, emanating from a place right over her outstretched fingertips, all the way to the street, forming a dome just big enough for the two of them. They could see through the bright white light to the shaken animals outside, and it cast a glow around them like a giant torch in the black night.

The large cougar that had tried to pounce on them had apparently bounced right off this shield of light. It and the others were walking around the circle of light, briefly stunned, but quickly regaining their confidence. One of the others charged them. Eliza kept her hands up and Jonah stayed still as the animal hit the outside of the shield and was thrown back, yelping in pain. The others began to roar, but none dared approach the circle of light around them.

Jonah caught his breath, looking back up at his sister. "How did you do *that*?"

Eliza grinned, hands still held high. "I—I don't know. . . . The cougar was jumping, and something inside me said, '*This is not going to happen.*' I just stood up and held my hands out. The next thing I knew, this happened." She nodded at the shield around them.

"Wow. I mean, seriously, Eliza. *Wow*." It was all he could say as they stood there, fully protected from the animals around them.

"Yeah." She smiled. "I guess I really am part angel, huh?"

"Quarter angel," he reminded her. "But that was . . . amazing. *A shield of light*. I can't even do that."

He distinctly saw her blushing in the light that shone around them.

"Now let's see if we can get out of here," said Jonah. He walked around to the edges of the shield, looking at it. He worked up the nerve to reach up his finger and touch one of the beams of light, expecting it to burn him. Instead, it felt cool, even soothing, when he touched it, and his finger pushed right through. "Awesome," he said. "Maybe it hurts them, but not us."

The yellow-eyed cougars were still circling, afraid of the shield but seemingly content to wait patiently.

"What should we do, Jonah?" Eliza asked. "We can't stay out here forever, and I don't think they are going away anytime soon."

Jonah nodded, looking beyond the cougars now, at the road ahead. "Look up there." He pointed. "There's a truck." About a hundred feet away, a yellow truck had been parked on the side of the road. "Can you walk and hold the shield up at the same time?"

"What are you going to do?" she asked. "Drive?"

He looked at her impatiently. "Just come on."

She moved her arms tentatively, and when the light bubble moved along with her, she began to walk, still holding her arms up. The circle of light followed wherever she went. The roaring cougars moved reluctantly out of the way as she approached. Jonah walked closely behind her so that they both remained within the shield's protection, and slowly they made their way to the truck.

It was a large yellow pickup with wooden sides that held tools on the outside. Mainly rakes and shovels. The workers had apparently left it overnight, thinking no one would bother it on a deserted stretch of road like this.

"I think this will do," Jonah said as they approached the

truck. "Stand a little closer, Eliza." She moved so close that the edge of the shield touched the side of the vehicle. Jonah unhooked a shovel from the rack, pulling it inside the shield, and gripped it in both hands.

"Ready?" he said to her. Eliza saw what he was planning and nodded, turning again to face the cougars. Jonah now stood in front of Eliza, and they walked in lockstep toward the animals, the shield still protecting them fully. When they got close enough, he swung the shovel out in front of them, in a wide arc, through the beams of light.

The first cougar was caught totally off guard. The bottom side of the shovel connected with the side of its skull, and the animal hit the ground, immediately knocked unconscious by the blow. It made Jonah feel sick to hurt an animal, especially when the awful thought hit him that maybe it wasn't the poor cougar's fault at all—maybe there was a fallen one controlling the cougar that was attacking them. Jonah remembered what Henry had called it—*Holding*. It made a shudder run down his spine, but what else could they do? Fighting them off was the only thing he could think of.

Jonah swung again and caught another one across the body, sending it yelping across the pavement. It lay motionless on the ground for a few seconds, then stood up, shook, and galloped toward the woods. The others were backing away now, as Jonah and Eliza came nearer. The large cougar was still there, not moving toward them, but still growling. Jonah swung one more time, hard, connecting with its rear end and sending it twenty feet in the air. It screeched like a kitten and scurried away into the trees. The rest of the cougars followed.

Jonah and Eliza watched the last one disappear into the trees.

When they were alone on the road, she finally dropped her arms. The shield disappeared, and the two of them stood in the dark again. They both folded their arms at the same time and stared at each other.

"Unbelievable," Jonah said, shaking his head.

But a huge grin erupted on Eliza's face, and she yelled, "That totally rocked!"

ELEVEN

THE TRAIN TO NEWARK

As quickly as they had celebrated, though, the reality of what happened hit them and they were back on their bikes, Jonah pedaling ferociously, Eliza hanging on for dear life.

They kept their eyes alert now, glancing back over their shoulders frequently. So far, nothing else had emerged from the woods or the road ahead. Finally, Jonah wheeled them up to the train station in downtown Peacefield, and they threw their bikes behind the bushes beside the parking lot, thinking that if they hid them, there would be a better chance of recovering them when they came back. *If we even make it back.* The thought hit him before he could ward it off. *Don't think like that, Jonah. We are going to make it. We have Elohim on our side.*

Eliza stuck extra close to him as they searched for the ticket counter. They purchased two tickets to Newark and then hurried to catch the train that had just pulled in.

Nervous from their experience on the road, Jonah and Eliza walked through two cars before they settled into seats. Jonah leaned his head back against the headrest, closing his eyes and taking a deep breath for the first time in hours. He was just glad they had made it onto the train and were finally safe. Eliza, however, couldn't control her energy as she sat beside him.

"I can't believe what just happened back there!" she said, beaming. "Did you see that? Did you see what came out of my fingers?"

"I was there, Eliza," said Jonah. "I saw everything."

She acted like she didn't even hear him. "They were coming at us, weren't they? They had us surrounded. And when that big cougar jumped, something inside of me said no way it's going to get us, because we are on a mission for Elohim, right? So my hands just flew up, and the next thing I knew, there's this . . . force field . . . of super-dense light particles or something . . . all around us. That big cat bounced right off!"

Gleefully, she continued on for another couple of minutes, and Jonah rested his chin on his fist, waiting for her to finish, or at least breathe. He had to admit, he was impressed with his little sister. He had extraordinary strength, and she could create a shield out of light. He wondered what else they could do.

The words were starting to come back to him, verses that Mrs. Aldridge had spoken right before they left, as they were standing in the doorway together.

"What was it she said?" he muttered, and then grabbed the little Bible she gave him from his pocket, turning to the bookmarked passage. "Put on the whole armor of God . . . that you may be able to stand against the wiles of the devil . . . taking the shield of faith with which you will be able to quench all the fiery darts of the wicked one . . ."

Eliza was still talking, but stopped abruptly when she heard the word *shield*.

"The 'shield of faith'! Of course," she said. "The verses Mrs. Aldridge read."

"Ephesians 6:10–17."

She grabbed the small book and read the passage for herself.

"Put on the whole armor of God. . . . For we do not wrestle against flesh and blood, but against . . . spiritual hosts of wickedness in the heavenly places . . . the breastplate of righteousness . . . having shod your feet . . . taking the shield of faith . . . the helmet of salvation . . . the sword of the Spirit . . ."

She considered the words for a minute. "You think these are all powers that we could really have? That this armor of God, it's actually . . . *real armor?*"

Jonah thought about that. "We are definitely in a battle against something bigger than just flesh and blood. Like Dad said, there is a spiritual battle going on that is more real than we ever would have guessed. And now we're in the thick of it. So, yeah, maybe this 'armor of God' stuff is a lot more real too. Mrs. Aldridge sure seemed to think so, didn't she? The way she looked at us . . ."

Jonah's voice trailed off.

"Do you think she knew where we were going?" asked Eliza.

"Yeah, I think she did," Jonah said. "I mean, it doesn't make any sense. How could she know? She's just an old church lady, right? But showing up in the middle of the night, telling us those Bible verses, I just got the feeling that she knew everything."

They both sat for a while in silence, thinking about everything that had happened in the last hour. Eliza looked down at her skinny fingers, squeezing them into fists, then opening them back up again, as if she couldn't quite believe that kind of power had come out of these hands.

"You know, Eliza," Jonah said, "you said that right before the cougar jumped, you felt a strong sense that nothing was going to hurt us, that you weren't going to let it happen. Then—*boom!*—a shield of light, protecting us from the animals."

Eliza let out a soft whistle. "Amazing."

"But the animals," Jonah said in a low voice. "That's the thing that scares me. They can control them. If they can use a pack of wild cougars to chase us down and almost kill us, imagine what else they can do." They sat in silence, considering hundreds of awful possibilities.

"Remember the story about Jesus and the pigs?" Eliza said. "Jesus sent the demons out of a guy and into a bunch of them. And then they ran right off a cliff and down onto the rocks below. Poor pigs."

"Yeah, I remember that one," said Jonah. "I used to sit in Sunday school and think that would be cool, to see a bunch of pigs fly off the edge of a mountain. Not after what we just saw, though. I don't want to see any more animals doing anything crazy."

"So they know," she said darkly. "Why else would they have sent the cougars? They must know that we left the house. And they probably know where we're going."

The train had begun to move, and both of them sank a little lower in their chairs. Dark outlines of buildings moved past them as the train gathered speed. The lights inside the train were not overly bright, but enough to see the faces of the other passengers. Jonah and Eliza began looking around at the people on the train, trying to catch glimpses of anyone who might look suspicious.

A pudgy man with a large briefcase at his feet was reading the paper two seats behind them. He was focused on the business section and didn't seem to notice Jonah when he turned around to look. One row behind him, a white-haired lady in a pink-flowered dress with huge glasses and a shawl around her shoulders was knitting something and humming. He snuck a peek ahead of them and saw a man in a black leather jacket four rows away, tapping his fingers on the side of his chair, headphones on his ears. His black hair was shaved into a Mohawk, and he was nodding to the beat. Beside him, two older teenagers, a boy and a girl, sat really close to each other, the boy whispering in her ear, the girl giggling uncontrollably.

Mohawk-man suddenly stood up and turned around. He had more face piercings than Jonah had thought was possible on one human being. Rings across both eyes, several in his lip and nose, although for some reason, none on his ears. Pulling his headphones down around his neck, he began walking down the aisle toward them.

"Eliza!" Jonah whispered, trying not to look too alarmed. He grabbed her leg and squeezed.

"Ow! What are you . . . ?" But as she looked up she saw him coming too. The pierced man kept moving their way, slowly, and looking right at them.

"Get ready," Jonah said, balling his hands into fists. The man had a chain coming out of his pocket that clattered against each seat he passed. He locked eyes with Jonah and Eliza, and his eyes grew beady and small. Finally standing right in front of them, he leaned down until he was no more than a couple of feet away. Jonah squeezed his fists tightly, about to jump out of his seat.

"You two kids have a problem?" His voice was high-pitched and squeaky, not at all what they expected coming from someone who looked so tough. They just stared at him, not sure how to answer. He squeaked again, "You're starin' at me. I don't appreciate people starin' at me."

Jonah loosened his fists. "Sorry, sir. We didn't mean to stare."

He gulped. "We've just never seen . . . never seen so many . . ." He made himself shut up, knowing he was going in the wrong direction. But the man suddenly grinned, showing three gold teeth.

"Never seen so many a 'ese?" he said, pointing over his eye to all the rings. "That's awright, kids. I get that all the time. People usually just jealous." He patted Jonah hard on the shoulder with a leather-gloved hand. "Maybe you kin have some a 'ese one day, huh? Now, which way's the men's room?"

Jonah and Eliza looked at each other as he walked on past, and when he had finally found the small bathroom at the back of the car, they burst out in muffled laughter.

"I can't wait to see your new eyebrow rings," Eliza said, snorting loudly.

Jonah elbowed her. "I'll get those as soon as you get your lip pierced five times."

The rest of the twenty-minute ride they loosened up, talking, giggling some more when Mohawk-man walked by again, quietly trying to figure out their plan once they got to New York. They were feeling better, even confident, about rescuing their mother. They were part angel, after all. And most important, Elohim was with them. He wanted them to succeed, and if He was with them, what did they have to fear?

But as soon as Jonah grew confident with that thought, another, more sinister one came. *Elohim was there when they took her. And He didn't do anything to stop them. Why was that?* This unsettled him, and he fidgeted in his seat the rest of the way to the station.

"Next stop is Newark Station," the computerized voice said over the loudspeaker.

They hopped off the train into a busy lobby and began looking for the subway they needed to ride into the city. Morning rush hour was a few hours away, but there were still plenty of people, compared to the lonely feeling of the Peacefield train station. People were hopping onto trains, scrambling toward exits, or looking for the next train to catch. Jonah and Eliza wove their way through the crowd, finally passing into a tunnel that led to the subway connection point. Jonah glanced up at the old clock. 3:47 a.m. They had just enough time to spare. The subway that would take them to the World Trade Center Station, on the south end of New York City, was scheduled to leave at four o'clock.

The brick tunnel was not very long, but dark and damp. Moss was growing on some of the bricks, water trickling down the sides, and Eliza shivered as they walked in. For a moment, they were away from the crowd, alone, footsteps echoing off the walls.

"Excuse me, young ones."

The shaky voice of an elderly woman came from behind them. They turned to see an old lady in a pink-flowered dress with a shawl over her shoulders, hunched over with a cane. The lady who had been on the train, sitting a few rows back. She smiled pleasantly as she held something out in her hands.

"Yes, ma'am?"

The old woman's hand trembled holding the paper. "I'm trying to find my way, and I have this map, but I just can't seem to read it." She laughed sweetly. "These old eyes ... I have these huge glasses and I still can't see a darn thing. Do you think you could help me out, honey?"

Eliza stepped forward helpfully, smiled at her, and took the map. "Of course. Where are you trying to go?"

Jonah watched them study the crumpled piece of paper. A slight breeze brushed against his face, and he shivered from a sudden chill. Deep down, a familiar feeling began to well up. The same feeling he'd experienced the other night, riding his bike on the dark road. Fear.

Something was wrong.

"Eliza!" He pulled her toward him. "I think we need to go."

"I'm just trying to help this lady, Jonah," she said, swatting at him while staring at the map. "Hold on a sec."

Jonah grabbed her arm. "Eliza! Listen to me. *We have to go.*"

She was about to let him have it when she saw the fear etched on his face. Eliza turned back and looked at the elderly woman.

She was still smiling that sweet, grandmother-like smile, but instead of hunching over, she now stood totally upright, and her eyes flashed sharp yellow in the shadows of the hallway. Her lips parted as her smile grew bigger, revealing gleaming, razor-sharp teeth that almost matched the yellow color of her eyes. She began to laugh.

"You didn't think you could get away from us that easily, now, did you? You may have outsmarted my cougars, yes, but we're not done with you yet." Holding her cane up like a sword, a long blade suddenly popped out from the end, along with two smaller blades on each side.

"Run!" Jonah yelled. Still holding Eliza's arm, he bolted toward the entrance to the subway station. But they heard a clattering sound and felt the brush of someone moving very quickly over their heads. The old woman fell from the ceiling, right in their path. Somehow she had scurried past them, like a spider on the wall, and blocked the exit. They stopped in their tracks, mouths hanging open.

"I may be old," she said, in her frailest voice. But then her voice changed, growing strong and low. "But I can still move pretty fast, don't you think?"

She glared at them in the darkness, her yellow eyes cutting through it, eyeing them like a spider toying with a couple of flies caught in her web. Suddenly, she charged at them, snarling, a crazed look on her face, with her cane-sword raised. She was too fast for them to run away.

Jonah did the only thing he knew to do. He stepped forward, and before she could swing the cane down toward them, he grabbed it with his left hand. With his right, he latched onto her other arm and pushed her as hard as he could.

She flew back against the brick wall with force and fell to the ground, dazed. His strength had caught her off guard. Within seconds, though, she sprang back up, barking at them through her sharp teeth.

"Pretty strong for a young boy, aren't you, sonny?" she cackled, throwing her head back violently. "I guess that's what happens when your mother is one of *us*." She smiled knowingly, nodding at them both.

"Our mother is *not* one of your kind," Eliza said boldly. "And she never will be!"

The old woman laughed hysterically and then croaked at them in that dark, low voice. "Oh yes, my dear, she will. In fact, she practically already is."

She came after them again, this time along the side of the wall, defying gravity as she scuttled across the bricks. But Eliza was ready for her. Her hands shot up, and a shield immediately formed around her and Jonah, just as the woman leapt at them. She hit the shield, screaming in pain, and bounced away onto the stone floor.

Jonah looked past her, down the tunnel and into the open subway station beyond. He knew the subway train would be leaving very soon, and they had to figure out a way to get on it. The old woman had picked herself up off the ground again, her smile now gone.

"Nice," the fallen one said, "very nice indeed, Eliza." Eliza jumped when she said her name, and the old woman began to pace in front of them. "Oh yes, we know your names. Jonah and Eliza Stone. And I believe you have a little brother, Jeremiah. Your mother, of course, we have already met." Eliza still held her hands high, and at the mention of her little brother, she returned the woman's glare with one of her own.

"The shield of faith, my young girl. Very impressive, very impressive indeed. Discovered your gifts all on your own, have you? You both have the hand of *Him* helping you, of course. That's obvious. How incredibly... disgusting." A drop of saliva dribbled onto her chin. By *Him*, Jonah knew she meant Elohim.

"You won't be able to hurt us, or even keep us here," he said, trying to keep his voice calm. "You and all of your fallen friends are no match for Elohim." At his name, the old woman shuddered, drawing back, hissing. But as she stood back up, she threw her hands toward the ceiling and produced a shield of her own, the color of crimson. It looked strong in the darkness of the tunnel.

With an evil grin, she began to advance toward them. Eliza continued to boldly hold her shield in place. Soon, though, the old lady was close enough that her shield touched Eliza's.

"Ahh!" shouted Eliza, her knees buckling underneath her. She still held her hands high, but she was being forced backward. "Help, Jonah! I don't know how long I can hold my arms up! Her shield is ... sapping my energy."

Eliza's shield was holding so far, but Jonah saw that its light was growing dimmer, while the red shield of the fallen one seemed to grow even stronger.

"I'm getting . . . really tired," Eliza said wearily.

Jonah grabbed her two arms and held them up, and momentarily the light began to shine brighter. "Come on, Eliza! You can do it! I'm here with you." But as soon as the shield strengthened, the old woman reared back and threw her full force into hers. Eliza screamed, and her hands suddenly dropped to her side. With an explosion, the shield disappeared, and they were catapulted into the air and onto their backs.

The woman grabbed her cane and began to walk across the room with it, slowly, ready to bask in the glow of their defeat.

"You really didn't think you would be any match for me, did you, now? You may have a few powers, but you certainly don't know how to use them." Her sweet-old-lady voice was back, and she looked as if she were no more harmful than any senior citizen enjoying a stroll with her grandchildren. "I've destroyed people much more skilled than you in my day."

Jonah had hit his head and felt that at any minute he might pass out. His vision was blurred, and he could barely make her out, hobbling over toward him.

He closed his eyes, not sure if he was dreaming or awake. A voice somewhere inside of him began to pray, *Elohim, help us. We need You. Show me what to do.*

As quickly as the words were said, he felt a tingling in his feet. His eyes snapped open again, and he was wide-awake. He saw the fallen one taking her time walking over to them, gloating in her victory, but his eyes were drawn to his feet. They continued to tingle, and he sat up. His white sneakers were starting to bubble, like boiling water in a pot. Jonah could not believe what he was seeing. His shoes were changing, morphing, right on his feet. And where his shoes used to be were now a pair of ancient-looking, brown leather sandals. His feet suddenly felt light. Lighter than they ever had before.

Quickly Jonah stood up, a new energy flowing through him. He picked up Eliza, who was still moving slowly, and held her by his side.

"It's time to go, E," he whispered in her ear as he kept his eyes on the fallen angel. Just as the old woman was reaching her bony hand out to snare them, he began to run. Holding Eliza with him, his feet blazed around her and up the side of the tunnel, just as she had done a minute ago. He heard the woman scream and the clatter of her own feet, trying to get in front of them again, but she was no match for Jonah's speed. They burst out and into the subway station area, a blast of light, leaving the echoing screams behind.

The subway doors had opened, and a crowd of people were pushing their way on. Jonah went straight for the closest open door. He slowed down and he and Eliza jumped inside together, just as the doors closed. Squirming past several people, they found two hard plastic seats and plopped themselves down.

Only then was Jonah able to look down at his feet. Eliza did too. But gone were the leather sandals. Back on his feet were his old white basketball shoes. He heard Mrs. Aldridge's voice reading the words of the Scriptures again, and he jolted upright in his seat.

"There was something else Mrs. Aldridge said . . ." Jonah was shaking in his seat, but he pulled out the Bible again. "Put on the whole armor of God . . . having shod your feet with the preparation of the gospel of peace . . ."

"*Shod* means that you get shoes put on you, like a horse," Eliza said. "There it is again—the verse coming to life."

They sat for a few minutes in silence, watching the lights of the tunnel pass by outside the subway car, flashing into the windows. Jonah wiggled his toes again, but they felt entirely normal. There was no other way to explain it. The words of the Bible passage were coming true.

Literally true.

"Your shield saved us again, Eliza," Jonah said.

"Yeah," she said quietly, crossing her arms and shivering, the reality of what had just happened starting to come over her. "But hers was stronger. I'm scared, Jonah. That was . . . absolutely awful." She looked away from him, out the window of the subway train. "How are we going to do this?"

"Don't you know we have angel blood in us?" Jonah said, hitting her on the arm. "The only reason we have made it this far is because Elohim is on our side. And if He is with us, there's nothing that's going to stop us."

She turned back toward him and nodded, managing a smile.

Jonah leaned his head back and looked toward the window, not wanting her to see any doubt in his eyes. He watched the darkness pass by outside and spent the next few minutes quietly hoping he was right.

TWELVE

A DARK ALLEYWAY

The subway clacked along the track quickly, the cold white lights the only thing shining in the underground tunnel. There were men and women standing and sitting all around them in the car, some going home from a late night on the town, some getting ready for another fast-paced day of work in the Big Apple.

Slowly Eliza said under her breath, "You know, every one of them could be . . . *like her.*"

Like her. The sweet-grandmother-looking lady was the last person on the train they would have suspected to be one of the Fallen. But now they realized that anyone could be working for Abaddon.

"Yeah, you're right. Any one of these people could be a fallen one. But you know what it also means?" he said, a new thought hitting him. "Any of them could also be an angel."

He felt crazy, glancing around out of the corner of his eyes, wondering who was human and who wasn't.

It was a twenty-minute ride to New York City, and no one seemed to be staring at them, no one looked ready to pounce at any moment. Maybe in a crowd they were actually safer than when they were alone.

"So what's the plan when we get to New York?" Eliza asked, brushing brown wisps of hair off her face.

Jonah looked down at the MissionFinder 3000. It appeared to be just like any other old, silver watch. He glanced around to see if anyone was watching and then pushed the button on the side. The orange screen glowed, but gave no new information.

"It says the same thing. We're supposed to go to New York City." He shrugged. "I guess we'll get more instructions when we get there."

They continued to hunch down in their seats, talking quietly with each other, wanting to do nothing to draw attention to themselves. Soon, a crackling voice came over the loudspeaker.

"World Trade Center Station. Next stop, World Trade Center Station."

They stepped out into the dimly lit station. Jonah looked at his watch again as people jostled by them. 4:21 a.m.

"We're here now," said Eliza, looking over his shoulder. "Let's see if it says anything more specific."

He pushed the button again. The orange screen flashed on, but this time two black letters filled the screen, blinking.

"HR," Jonah said slowly, showing it to Eliza. "HR? What does that mean?"

"Push the button again," she said. He did, and the old watch screen returned. Jonah tried pressing it again, but this time nothing happened.

"Hey, what's wrong with this thing?" He shook his arm and tried again. It was no use. The screen stayed the same.

"HR . . . HR . . . HR . . ." Eliza turned the letters over in her brain. "Is that some kind of message? A secret code? Did Marcus say anything about that?"

Jonah thought hard. "I can't remember anything."

"Well, he must have said something," she said, growing frustrated. "Think hard, Jonah."

"I'm trying! And I'm telling you, they didn't mention anything about HR or any kind of secret code. It just said we'd get more specifics when we got here."

They were stumped.

Eliza paced around him in the terminal. "What are we supposed to do now?"

He could think of nothing else to do. "I say we just . . . walk."

Since she had no better ideas, they left the lobby and exited onto a noisy street full of taxicabs and a growing number of pedestrians.

"I guess we'll figure it out, right?" Eliza said, trying to sound confident as she huddled down in her hoodie.

"Right."

Jonah's legs were beginning to feel like cold noodles, but he pushed forward and tried to ignore them. With each step, though, the fact that they had no plan was hitting him in the face. *"Show up in New York City and figure it out from there"* felt brave back in Peacefield. Now it just seemed plain stupid.

They walked east, looking for a sign, a gut feeling, anything that might point them in the right direction. The farther they walked, the more the busy streets began to thin out. Suddenly, Eliza stopped, staring up at a traffic light. Jonah quickly realized she wasn't looking at the light itself, but at what was on top of it.

Across the steel bar that held the stoplights up at the busy intersection of Wall Street and Water Street sat two angels.

"Look at that," Jonah said, as they both stared at the stunning creatures. Eliza nodded slowly, her mouth open, mesmerized. One was male, the other female, and they sat high above the traffic. Their massive wings filled the air behind them, shimmering with a white light and rustling in the breeze.

Jonah looked around at the people passing them by. Apparently no one could see the angels but them. According to Henry, humans could not see an angel unless the angel wanted them to. But watching these people move so hurriedly up and down the street, he wondered if they would stop to look even if they *could* see them.

"Look, Jonah!" said Eliza. "They're waving!"

Not only that, but like an Olympic gymnast, the male angel whirled around the bar over and over again and then let go, propelling himself into the air, so high that Jonah quickly lost sight of him. After a few seconds, Eliza said, "Look!" and they saw him zooming down, headfirst, toward the street below. At the last second, he reached out and grabbed the steel bar again, flipped around it one more time, and landed back beside his counterpart. He bowed dramatically, winking at them. His friend rolled her eyes but laughed at him, and they waved at Jonah and Eliza again.

"Wow," Eliza whispered. "They're beautiful."

The angels hopped down to the other side of the street, across from them, and beckoned them to come over. Jonah and Eliza looked at each other, Eliza nodded eagerly, and they waited to cross the street. When the light had turned red and the cars speeding by them stopped, they made their way across.

"My name is Robert," the tall one with the dark hair said with a friendly smile.

"And I'm Helene," the woman said, smiling, looking deep into Jonah's eyes. Eliza stared up at them both, captivated.

"Helene. Robert. HR!" Jonah exclaimed. "You must be who we're looking for."

"I . . . I . . ." Eliza tried to speak but no words came.

Robert laughed loudly. "Cat got your tongue, Eliza?"

She just nodded stupidly, still speechless. Jonah would normally have been amused by his sister's sudden lapse in brainpower, but, after all, these *were* the most good-looking angels they had ever seen.

"Let's cut to the chase," Robert said, grinning and winking at them both. "Are you ready to see your mother?"

"You know where she is?" Jonah asked eagerly.

Helene reached out and touched his arm. "Of course, Jonah. She is safe. But she needs you. She needs you both."

"We've been waiting for you all night," Robert said. "We're glad you finally made it. Let's take you to your mother."

They began walking down a street that was almost completely deserted and much darker. The sun still hadn't risen, and it was especially dark among the tall buildings. Helene turned and motioned to them to follow, still smiling warmly.

"Come on, Jonah!" Eliza said, following them. "They're going to take us to get Mom!"

Jonah paused as he caught Helene's eyes again. There was something . . . the way she was looking at him, unblinking . . . A small voice deep within him was trying to speak to him, one he could barely hear above the noise of the street and his own heartbeat. Something was trying to hold him back, warning him, tugging at his soul. But these were angels, and the prospect of having his mother back was louder than whatever quiet voice was trying to speak to him inside. This had to be the next step, the one they were looking for.

"Jonah!" Eliza beckoned impatiently. "*Hurry up.*"

Robert and Helene walked briskly. Jonah and Eliza struggled to keep up, half-walking, half-running to make sure they didn't fall too far behind. Jonah became aware of the putrid smell of rotting garbage as they made their way down the street.

Robert finally stopped. "This is the way we have to go," he said. All they could see of the angels were their eyes, gleaming in the shadows. He pointed into the darkness of a narrow passage off the alleyway.

"In . . . there?" Eliza swallowed hard.

"Yes, of course," Helene said, a slight edge to her syrupy voice. "This is where the door is, to get inside and find your mother. Come on, now. Hurry along. She's very close."

Shivering and covering their noses, Jonah and Eliza peered into the crevice between two buildings. They could make out the outlines of a few metal doors and a rusted-out staircase that went up along the side of one of the walls. Jonah could tell Eliza was nervous, but she managed to smile at Robert and Helene, and took a brave step into the alleyway.

The smell grew even stronger. It was horrible, and yet also vaguely familiar . . .

"Someone forgot to empty the garbage," Robert with a chuckle that seemed rather forced. "Come on now, Jonah. We don't want to keep your mother waiting any longer, do we?"

Jonah shook his head, catching Helene's eyes again as he walked by. For the briefest moment, he thought he saw a glimmer of . . . yellow.

Yellow eyes. The same ones he had seen just an hour ago, in the Newark terminal. The same ones he had seen just a few hours before, on a lonely stretch of highway in Peacefield. And the same ones he had seen in the face of the hideous creature that chased him all the way to Mrs. Aldridge's house.

Helene and Robert weren't the "HR" after all. Jonah was suddenly sure about that.

He was moving to grab Eliza's hand and pull her back through the alley when he realized that Robert and Helene were standing in the entrance, blocking their way back to the street. Closing off any escape route they would have. Jonah began to move away from them as Eliza turned around.

"What's going on, guys?" she said, and then gasped.

In front of them, the angels were changing. The glow of their yellow eyes grew stronger in the darkness. Their faces were turning dark, almost black. They had been standing straight up, tall and strong, but now they began to hunch over, like someone carrying a heavy burden on his shoulders. Their wings crumpled, blackening, as if they had been set on fire and then extinguished. They grew sharp and angular behind their backs. Gone were their crisp white clothes, replaced by dark leathery skin that looked like armor. Their fingers grew long, with sharp claws on the end. Yellowish teeth protruded from their mouths now, crooked and vicious. They stood in the darkness, glaring at the two kids in front of them.

The one who had called himself Robert spoke, a sarcastic tone in his hissing voice, which had changed along with his appearance. "Didn't your mother tell you to never trust a fallen angel?"

Helene reached back over her shoulder and in her hand appeared a long arrow, flaming red at the tip. A bow was suddenly in her other hand, and she strung the arrow as she spoke. "It's time for both of you to go away. Forever." In an instant, Robert had pulled and strung a flaming arrow too, and they trained them on Jonah and Eliza.

They turned and ran as fast as they could down the alleyway. An arrow flew just over Eliza's shoulder, slamming into the wall beside her. It disappeared like black dust into the brick, but the wall erupted in flames. The one aimed at Jonah grazed his hair, exploding into a pile of garbage in a corner of the street. Flames shot up into the sky as the trash caught fire.

Eliza quickly moved behind a pair of garbage cans, dropping out of sight. Jonah's closest shelter was a small Dumpster, and he scurried to get behind it. They both crouched down against metal and the cold street, and Jonah saw Eliza's terrified eyes trying to locate him in the dark.

The Fallen were walking slowly down the alleyway. He could sense it even though he had not turned around to look. For the briefest moment, he closed his eyes, gathering himself. He glanced at Eliza again. She had located him in the darkness and was watching him, looking back over her shoulder, and waiting.

String your bow, Jonah.

The words came out of nowhere, and he wasn't sure if they had been spoken out loud or were just in his mind. But he heard them clearly, and in one motion, before another thought ticked across his brain, he stood up, turned toward the fallen ones, and reached back over his shoulder. An arrow appeared in his right hand, and then suddenly there was a bow in his left. The arrow was on fire with a pure white flame on the tip, and as it passed by his face he felt a cool sensation hit him, not heat.

This shook Eliza out of the shock she was in. She quickly sprang up, standing alongside her brother, and threw her hands up above her. Beams of white light erupted from her fingertips, forming a shield around them both, as they stood back to back in the alleyway. All of this happened at once, before the Fallen had even had a chance to blink. Then Jonah aimed the arrow at Robert and fired. It pierced Eliza's shield easily, moving through it as if nothing were there.

Robert ducked his head, and the white flaming arrow flew past him and hit a trash can. A flash of white light blasted the can all the way out of the alley and across the street. Robert looked back at it, clearly surprised. He turned back toward them both, looking even angrier than before. Both he and Helene began to fire arrows, one after the other. But every time they hit the shield, they evaporated into dust. Jonah kept pulling arrows off his back, aiming them, and letting them go. They were faster than he was, though, and they kept avoiding his shots. Plus, his aim was not very good.

"Will you please hit them?" Eliza begged, her voice straining as she concentrated on the shield.

Jonah was firing arrow after arrow, but kept missing. "I'm trying! These guys are faster than they look!"

"I think you need to work on your aim, Jonah!" Robert shouted, as he rolled against the wall, dodged another arrow, and fired his own black arrow into the shield. Jonah immediately shot one that hit no more than an inch from his head. Closer. Robert growled and dove to the ground.

He was having a hard time focusing on both of them at once, and that was probably how Helene got so close without him realizing it. But suddenly, while Jonah was trying to get a good shot on Robert, she had rolled forward on the ground and stood up, right in front of Eliza. She contorted her face into a yellow-toothed grin with her sharp teeth and raised her hand to her face, holding it flat, just in front of her lips. There was something on the palm of her hand.

"Jonah!" Eliza yelled, and he turned, but it was too late. Helene blew across her open hand, and something dusty and black floated in the air toward her. When it hit the shield, Eliza screamed in pain, and she staggered back and down on her knees. The shield flickered a couple of times, and then went out.

They were exposed. Whatever that dust was, it was strong enough to extinguish the shield when it touched it. All Jonah and Eliza could do was try to scramble backward as fast as they could. Both of the fallen ones held flaming arrows up to their bows, Robert's aimed at Jonah, Helene's at Eliza.

"Good-bye, children," Robert said calmly.

Jonah could hear his heart beating furiously in his ears, and the likelihood that he was going to die crossed his mind. He would never see his mother, his father, or his brother again. Closing his eyes, he waited for the arrow to pierce his heart.

Suddenly, a blur of light came from over the top of the building, right above the fallen ones. Jonah's eyes popped open, and the fallen ones turned and looked up, only to find the charging bullet of light coming directly for them. Before they could think of shielding themselves, the blur crashed into them both, blasting them into the alleyway wall, sending shards of bricks and a cloud of dust flying through the air.

The fallen angels fell to the ground, covered in rubble. Something, or someone, grabbed their arms, and Jonah and Eliza began to rise quickly into the sky. As they zoomed up next to the wall of the building and over the edge, Jonah saw Robert take off after them.

Jonah was on one side of whatever was carrying them, and Eliza on the other, hurtling through the air at an unbelievable rate of speed. They caromed around like a pinball, turning, ducking, diving around buildings, swerving narrowly to avoid streetlights. Jonah's head was bouncing back and forth as he flew along on his back, something wrapped around his arm tightly. But not painfully, Jonah realized. Finally, he was able to turn his head enough to see someone between the two of them wearing jeans and a white T-shirt, with two wings coming out of his back.

"Hi, Jonah!" The smiling face of Henry turned toward him briefly. "Having a good flight so far?"

All Jonah was able to say was, "*Aghhhhhhhhhhhhhhhhhhhh!*" Henry just laughed good-naturedly and readjusted his grip on Jonah's arm.

"Hold on, now, we've almost lost them," he said, gunning forward even faster as he circled building after building. Eliza was screaming at the top of her lungs. But after Jonah stopped panicking so much, he noticed that he didn't feel like he was being dragged. His body was not hanging down so much as it was floating along, with the angel. His feet and legs felt light. It was almost like with Henry holding on to him, he was able to fly too.

With no sign of the fallen angels, Henry began to descend. They floated toward the ground, in between a few large skyscrapers, landing in the median of a quiet street. Taxicabs were cruising past them, but there was no sign of the black creatures. They sensed something behind them, though, something large, and quickly Jonah and Eliza spun around. A giant bull with massive horns glared at them, looking like it was ready to charge.

"Ahhh!" Eliza yelled, and started to throw her hands up and form another shield as Jonah reached behind him for another arrow.

"Guys!" Henry said, trying not to break down in laughter. "It's a statue. You know, the Wall Street bull?"

They lowered their arms slowly, realizing that it was indeed a bronze statue of a bull. It looked menacing, but it wasn't going to charge after them anytime soon.

Jonah snorted as the tension drained from his limbs and laughter replaced it. Soon, he and Henry were laughing so hard that Jonah had to sit down on the sidewalk. When they finally stopped gasping for air, they found Eliza staring at them furiously.

"You about got us *killed*!" she said, pointing at Henry, whose smile faded just a little. "All of that flying around, every which way, zooming around buildings, up and down. Are you crazy?"

Jonah stepped forward. "He saved our lives, Eliza! What did you think was going to happen back there? Did you think those arrows were going to miss us again?"

"Hmph," mumbled Eliza, kicking the sidewalk at her feet.

Henry extended his hand, smiling warmly at her. "Hi, Eliza. I'm Henry. In all of the hubbub, we didn't get properly introduced back at your house. Glad you can finally see me, after all these years."

Reluctantly, she reached out and shook the angel's hand. "So how did you know where we were?"

"Henry is our family's guardian angel," Jonah answered, putting up his hand for Henry to high-five. "He can find us anytime he wants to."

"Guardian angel for our family, huh?" Eliza said. "Well, you haven't done a great job lately, have you? Our mom is gone, and this is the third time we've almost been killed today. And the sun's not even up."

And with that, she spun around and walked away. Jonah was about to go after her, but Henry grabbed his arm.

"No, Jonah," he said, watching her walk. "It's okay. Give her a minute. She's safe as long as we can see her. Anyway, I've been thinking the same thing myself, especially after today. It's just that, with you guys, well, there's been a lot going on, a lot of bases to cover. And at some point, even angels just have to trust Elohim." They sat in silence another minute, letting Eliza have her space. Finally, Henry got to his feet.

"Come on," he said to Jonah. "We need to get inside somewhere, get some breakfast, and find a private place where we can talk."

He began to walk after Eliza.

"And I think I know a spot."

THIRTEEN

Fraunces Tavern

Jonah, Eliza, and Henry hurried down the New York City street, and Jonah could tell that she was slowly softening toward the guardian angel. They continued to search the sky above them for any sign of the fallen angels, but apparently they really had lost them, at least for now. As they were about to round the corner and move onto a busier street, Henry paused.

"Hold on a second," he said, and moved into the shadows. He closed his eyes tight, and suddenly his wings disappeared. "Now there will be three of us, not just two."

"You mean people can see you now?" Eliza asked, her curiosity about Henry growing greater than her frustration. "Angels can do that? They can just make themselves appear and disappear?"

"Sure," he said, as they turned the corner. "Haven't you ever heard of people seeing angels?"

Eliza thought for a moment. "In the Bible, yes," she said. "But in real life? No. Not so much."

"If anything," Henry said, "I would think that your recent

experiences have proven that the same things that happened in the Scriptures can, and do, happen today."

They tried to stay in the darker shadows along the busy street as they talked.

"It just seems different, somehow," Eliza admitted. "Stuff that happened in the Bible all seems so amazing—God speaking to people in burning bushes, sick people touching Jesus and getting healed, angels all over the place, announcing things, protecting people—but it's not really the kind of stuff you hear about today, you know? At least not for *real*."

Henry smiled. "Maybe you haven't been looking in the right places."

Jonah's brow wrinkled. "What do you mean, Henry?"

"Well, you humans always think that if you can't see it, it's not happening," Henry explained. "That if it isn't happening to you, it must not be going on with anybody. But these last few days, you have clearly witnessed the power of Elohim like you never have before, right?"

They both nodded their agreement, and he continued.

"Humans today have a tough time understanding that there is a whole other world out there. That there are things going on all the time—battles, victories, defeats—between the forces of good and evil, that directly impact what you see and feel. There are no accidents, no coincidences. Everything that happens, both good and bad, has been caused by something else. And everything that happens has a purpose."

"Everything, Henry?" Jonah questioned. "Isn't that kind of hard to believe? What about things you can't explain? Like earthquakes that wreck whole cities and kill thousands of people, or when a kid gets kidnapped, or when a really great person dies from a heart attack?" *Or when your mother gets taken from you by evil men*, he thought.

Henry met his gaze with his clear, blue eyes. "Everything, Jonah—and I mean *everything*—passes through Elohim's hands before it is experienced by a human being. You can choose to believe that or not, but it doesn't make it any less true."

"You mean that Elohim causes these awful, evil things to happen?" Eliza erupted. "What kind of God is He? Why would He do that?" Her cheeks were flushed red, and both Jonah and Henry saw the emotion in her eyes and on her face. Jonah had never heard her ask those kinds of questions. But then again, they'd never had a lot of conversations about God before.

Henry stopped walking outside a brightly lit restaurant, shoved his hands deep in his pockets, and leaned against the window.

"That's the question," he responded quietly to Eliza, "that has stopped humans in their tracks from trusting and believing in Elohim for years and years. It has led many to a life of doubt, not faith. Here's the thing. You talk about Elohim causing these things to happen. Those fallen angels we just encountered? They used to be Elohim's holy angels, just like me. But they rebelled under His loving authority. They left heaven. Led by the darkest one—Abaddon himself. Do you know why?"

Jonah shrugged.

Eliza searched the database in her mind for the right answer. "They wanted to be better than Him," she said. "Greater than Elohim Himself."

Henry nodded, watching the traffic flow by, a detached look on his face. Like he was remembering something from long ago. "They chose to rebel. Those days were . . . well, dark. There was a battle across the heavens, unlike anything you have ever seen here." Henry swept his eyes across an imaginary horizon. Finally snapping himself out of his memory, he turned toward Eliza. "The point is, they chose this path. It was one of the most shocking things to occur in all of the angelic realm."

"That they chose to leave Elohim?" Jonah asked.

"That He *let* them choose to leave, Jonah," Henry said, grimacing. "And leave they did."

Eliza pushed her hair out of her face. "Why would He do that? Why didn't He just make them obey? He could. I mean, He is Elohim. He can do whatever He wants to. How could He let that happen?"

Henry answered her frustration softly. "That is the point I wanted to make, Eliza. He lets people—and angels, for that matter—make choices: to follow Him, or not; to obey Him, or go a different direction. These choices have consequences, and the more severe the choice, the more severe the consequences. They are just built into the system. And the most extreme choice of all is to rebel on purpose against Elohim. So those choices, well, they have the most extreme consequences."

Jonah felt something connect in his mind for the first time. "So you are saying that the evil, awful things that happen in our world are because someone chose to rebel against Elohim?"

"Yes, you could say that," Henry responded. "When this rebellion left the heavens and entered the earth, and people began to choose against the way of Elohim, those choices brought with them consequences. Look at it this way—the bad choices caused the world to break. And not only people, but our earth itself."

Eliza spoke up again. "So natural disasters, sickness and disease, evil—"

"All ultimately caused by rebellion against Elohim," Henry said.

"So maybe He doesn't cause these things to happen," she said, "but you still haven't said why He lets them go on."

"The answer to that question is all about faith," said Henry. "Believing that there is a grander plan that you haven't seen but that Elohim has, that He is working out. When you see one or two things that are happening, in reality He is doing thousands of things you cannot possibly see, or even understand. He allows us to make choices, and sometimes bad choices are made, making bad things happen. But even when bad things happen, He uses them for His purposes. He is so amazing," Henry said, awe in his voice. "You can know Him so closely, and yet there are so many things that are still a mystery."

The sign on the corner of the building said FRAUNCES TAVERN. Henry pushed open the door to the restaurant and held it open for them.

"Even for angels like you?" Jonah asked as they walked through.

Henry nodded, winking at him. "Even for me, Jonah."

The smell of bacon on the grill wafted through the door. Dark, old wood covered the tavern floor, and the weathered brick walls made the room feel warm and inviting. Fraunces Tavern was crammed full of men and women in business suits, sitting at tables, eating eggs and bagels and drinking coffee.

"Back there," Henry said, spotting a far corner booth that was empty. "Let's go."

The three worked their way over to the corner, sliding around the close tables, Henry offering "excuse me's" to people who didn't seem to be listening.

Finally they sat down, and a waitress came by and slid three waters in front of them.

"Drinks?" the waitress asked.

Soon, she was back with three tall glasses of orange juice for Jonah, Eliza, and Henry. The guys each ordered plates of eggs, bacon, and hash browns; Eliza asked for a bagel and cream cheese. Henry sat with his back to the wall and kept a cautious eye on the door.

"Aren't you supposed to keep up with us, Henry?" Jonah said, sipping his drink through a straw, thinking about the last attack. "You know, wherever we go, you're there?"

Henry wriggled uncomfortably in his chair. "Yes, Jonah, that's true. Guardian angels are there to help and assist. But I am splitting my time between you two and your dad and little brother at home. Jeremiah is a target for the Fallen too. So far they don't seem to have made a move for him yet. And I just . . . didn't anticipate that you'd be attacked so early in your mission. It would be horrible to lose you two. And it sure wouldn't help with . . ."

Jonah and Eliza waited for him to continue.

"Help with what?" Eliza finally asked.

He tapped his fingers on the table. "My promotion," he finally said.

"Angels can get promoted?" she said, leaning across the table with her eyes opened wide. "Like, getting your wings or something?"

Henry laughed, glancing over his shoulder. "I have those now, don't I? But something like that.

"So I see that you both are finding your gifts to be helpful," he said, quickly changing the subject. "Nice job back there with the shield, Eliza." Jonah thought he saw her blushing again.

"Did you have any run-ins before you got to New York?"

Jonah and Eliza looked at each other. Jonah launched into the story of their trip. They were both embarrassed that they hadn't recognized the fallen angels in the alley.

"I was . . . mesmerized by them," she said, lowering her eyes to the table, wishing she hadn't trusted them so easily.

"You will learn to use your instincts to discern the Fallen," said Henry. "It just takes time. The Scriptures are very clear that fallen ones can masquerade as angels of light quite convincingly. I'm not surprised they used that tactic against you."

Jonah grumbled. "I just wish I could have shot those arrows a little straighter. Maybe I would have hit one of them."

"I think I can help with that," he said.

Jonah wondered what he meant, but the waitress came back, so he didn't say anything. She slid the plates in front of them.

"I know you two are hungry," Henry said. "You'd better dig in."

Jonah heard his own stomach grumble, and suddenly it seemed like he hadn't eaten in days. He pounced on the stack of bacon while Eliza snatched a bagel from her plate, smothering it in cream cheese. Henry looked on.

"Aren't you going to eat?" Eliza asked him.

Henry held up a spoonful of egg. "Angels don't eat. This is just for show."

"Your loss," Jonah said and took another huge bite of bacon.

As Jonah ate, and Henry watched, images of his mother flashed in his mind, and even though he didn't want it to, his mind began to conjure up awful possibilities. Was she trapped in a room somewhere, banging on the door, trying to escape? Or held down with chains to the ground, exhausted from fighting the Fallen, having given up on the prospect of rescue? Maybe she was unconscious, barely alive, as they demanded loyalty to their side, committing her to a life of darkness and evil. Could she resist them this long? What did they want with her? Why did they need her so badly?

Or perhaps it was . . . worse. She was already one of them, programmed to do Abaddon's bidding. Like some kind of nephilim robot, awaiting his next command.

There was only one other option he could think of, and it was the one thing he really didn't want to think about.

Maybe she was already dead.

He suddenly wasn't hungry anymore. Dropping the food onto his plate, he pushed back from the table. "So where is Mom, and when are we going to get her back?"

He didn't care about the edge in his voice. The more he pictured what might be happening to her, the faster he wanted to get out of Fraunces Tavern, face whomever and whatever they had to, and bring her home. He looked at Henry intently.

"She is nearby. That is all we know," Henry said. "Marcus and Taryn received intelligence reports just before I came after you that gave us a very good estimation of where she was taken. It must be a location not very far from here."

Jonah stood up from the booth. "Well, what are we waiting for? Let's go!"

Henry held his hand up. "Sit back down for a minute, Jonah. You are eager to get her back, and so am I. But there are some things that you have to understand about where we are going. So that when we get there—*if* you can get there—you will know what we are up against."

Jonah slumped back down into his chair. "*If*? What's that supposed to mean?"

Henry cleared his throat. "Your mother is being held in a place that your father, for instance, could never have found. It's likely this has something to do with the mission being given to you."

"Because he's fully human?" Eliza asked.

"Exactly. Someone like your father, with great spiritual sensitivity, can sense the spiritual world, even if he cannot see it. For example, he can feel fallen angels' presence, their darkness. But he cannot *see* them, unless they choose to reveal themselves to him. Marcus, Taryn, me—we have allowed Benjamin to see us."

"But we can see the Fallen," said Jonah, "because we are quarterlings."

Henry nodded.

"So what exactly do they want with my mother?" Jonah asked, the question almost exploding out of him. "I heard what Marcus said. About how powerful nephilim are. And how they can be . . . swayed."

"There are so many things that hang in the balance here. Your mother and the other nephilim are the linchpin to their plan, and if they fall . . ." Henry paused. "Then I am afraid that everything all our futures hold will be in question. Abaddon has planned this for some time. He asked his fallen angels to father children—to create these nephilim."

While they were talking, Jonah paid the bill, and they headed out of the restaurant and down the street.

"Why would he want to create so many nephilim in the first place?" asked Jonah.

"Nephilim are immensely powerful creatures," Henry said. "They have a history of wreaking havoc on this earth. Marcus told you that they were part of what caused Elohim to send the flood in Noah's day. There is something about the combination of angel and human blood that makes them incredibly powerful, and quite unstable. Your mother has no idea what she is capable of. Of course, what we now know is that the birth of your mother was only one part of their plan."

Jonah walked in silence along with Eliza, his brain churning. This was so much bigger than just getting their mother back.

"Abaddon wants to use her to somehow rule the world?" Eliza asked.

"In some ways, he does rule this world," Henry said darkly. "What he wants is total rebellion and utter chaos. He wants hate, murder, selfishness. Those things cause him to grow stronger. He believes he can sway the nephilim to his side."

Henry continued to walk like he knew where he was going, turning another corner.

"There were others who were created and captured, as you know," he continued. "Seven others in all. Marcus and Taryn believe that they were all taken to the same place."

"They're all in New York together?" Eliza said. "Along with our mom?"

Henry nodded.

"Abaddon will try to break them down, to pull them into his grip and draw them into the war against Elohim. As you might imagine, he can be quite persuasive. One nephilim wields enormous power. They are great warriors. Having eight on their side—well, the world has never seen it. With their sheer strength and ability to influence humans, it would be no exaggeration to say that they could cause unprecedented destruction."

Jonah's brow furrowed. "What I don't get is that if Elohim knows all of this, why doesn't He just send down, like, a couple hundred thousand warrior angels to handle it? Why doesn't He just swoop in and take control and get our mother back?" Eliza nodded in agreement.

"It does no good to question the will of Elohim," Henry replied. "Send in warrior angels He may, and if He does, thanks be to Him. But our duty is to obey, to respond to what is in front of us, and to do our best to do what is right."

Jonah was not satisfied with that answer. He wanted to see power and strength, to watch the bad guys get destroyed. How was that going to happen through a ragtag couple of kids and a measly *guardian* angel?

"Where are we going, anyway?" Eliza said as she tried to keep up with the fast-moving Henry.

"There's another reason your dad would have failed in his attempt to get your mother back," he said. "You see, humans can't enter the hidden realm."

Eliza walked along silently for a few steps, squinting her eyes in thought. "Hidden realm? HR!" She pointed to Jonah's MissionFinder 3000.

Jonah held up the watch. "Since Helene and Robert didn't work out, I guess that makes perfect sense."

"Yes," said Henry. "Your mother and the other nephilim are located there."

Henry stopped walking. They had emerged from the shadows of the skyscrapers to the edge of a large lawn, almost the size of a football field, but rounder, with trees scattered through it. There were a few people sitting on benches. A lady in a pale green business suit was walking a tiny dog across the lawn.

Beyond the grass was an expanse of water, and in the middle of it, a small island with a figure just barely visible through a bank of fog under the cloud-choked sky.

"Look, Jonah!" Eliza pointed. "The Statue of Liberty!"

"Cool," he said. They were at the very southern tip of Manhattan.

They walked with Henry to the middle of the park and stood underneath the outstretched branches of a tree.

"The hidden realm is not so much a *where* as it is a *what*," Henry said, eyeing them both. "Jonah, pull out your Bible. Read Ephesians 6:12."

Jonah slid the book out of his pocket and found the verse.

"For we do not wrestle against flesh and blood, but against principalities, against powers, against the rulers of the darkness of this age, against spiritual hosts of wickedness in the heavenly places."

"Thank you," said Henry. "You see, there is a world that is invisible to humans. It's a layer, a deeper layer, to this physical world." He pointed to the people sitting on the bench across the lawn. "It's a world that most people do not believe exists. Even though they are influenced by it every day."

"Can humans see it—if they believe in it?" Eliza asked.

Henry smiled. "Insightful question, Eliza. They cannot see it like angels, who do most of their work there. But if they are in tune with it, they can sense it and even engage in the battle."

"How about us?" asked Jonah. "What about quarterlings?"

Henry cleared his throat. "In theory, since you have one-quarter angel blood, you should be able to access the hidden realm like any angel could."

"In theory? What does that mean?"

"I've never actually worked with quarterlings before," Henry admitted. "I don't know any angels who have. We're in some unknown territory here."

Suddenly, an image of Jonah's mother seared across his brain, a picture of her in chains, her exhausted face drooping, her eyes closed. He didn't know if it was just his imagination or for real.

"Let's try," Jonah said urgently. "What do we need to do to enter the hidden realm? How do you do it?"

"We just . . . do it. Angels don't think about it," Henry said, scratching his head. "But if I were to break it down, there are two things that allow us to enter the hidden realm. One is the fact that we are angels."

"Okay, we have that covered," said Eliza. "What's the second thing?"

"Belief. That a hidden realm exists, that you have always sensed, always been a part of, but never seen. That's the essence of faith, after all. Believing in what you don't see."

Jonah looked at Eliza. "Okay. Belief. We can do that."

Henry nodded. "Okay, then. All it should take is a heartfelt prayer."

Standing underneath the tree, he grabbed their hands so that they formed a circle and he closed his eyes.

Jonah caught Eliza's eye, and they both bowed their heads.

"Elohim, I believe in the reality of a spiritual world, which is the real world, where the battle between good and evil is taking place." Henry solemnly uttered these words and squeezed Jonah's hand.

Jonah cleared his throat and said from his heart, "Uh, I believe too."

"So do I," Eliza said.

They waited a few seconds, and then opened their eyes.

PART III

THE HIDDEN REALM

He reveals deep and hidden things; he knows what

lies in darkness, and light dwells with him.

Daniel 2:22 NIV

FOURTEEN

ARCHERY LESSONS

The first things Jonah noticed after he opened his eyes were Henry's wings. They were back again, sparkling with a silvery light much brighter than when he'd seen them earlier.

The second thing he noticed was Eliza. There was a glow emanating from her, a soft, brilliant golden light that seemed to be coming from the center of her chest and working its way out to her arms and feet, almost dripping off the ends of her fingertips.

Henry noticed Jonah and Eliza staring at each other. "It is the mark of Elohim you see. In the hidden realm, the true spiritual nature of people is much more evident. You have both given your hearts over to Him, allowing Him entrance into your lives. It's His light that shines through you. Quite beautiful, don't you think?"

Jonah reached out and touched Eliza on the arm, noticing the soft light around his own hand.

"Cool," he said under his breath. The glow around her was stunning. Eliza seemed just as mesmerized by the light coming from him, staring with a suprised smile.

Jonah sensed movement behind him and he turned quickly to see what it was. The woman who had been walking her dog had circled back and was on the path, staring right at them. The little fluffy dog seemed to be eyeing them too, and he growled and then barked.

"Max!" she said, tugging at his leash. "What's wrong, my little mushy-kins?" The dog just kept barking at them.

Jonah whispered to Henry, "Can she . . . ?"

"No," he said evenly. "She can't see us. Max the dog can't either. However, he can sense our presence. Dogs are funny like that."

"Elohim is Elohim." Jonah shrugged with a grin. He stepped forward until he was only a few feet away from the dog lady and waved. She looked straight through him and continued walking. He realized too late that he had gotten so close that he couldn't get out of the way in time. Bracing himself for a collision, he closed his eyes.

The woman passed right through him. Literally. Her entire body went through his. As this happened, Jonah felt a shock run through his chest, like a sudden blast of electricity. She must have felt the same thing, because she breathed in sharply, stopped in her tracks, and turned around. Her forehead wrinkled and her eyes looked longingly through Jonah once again, as if she had remembered something very important but had just as quickly forgotten it.

"Hmm," she said to herself, slowly turning away. They watched her continue to walk for a few more seconds.

"In the hidden realm, humans cannot see, hear, or touch you," Henry observed. "But every once in a while, they can sense your presence."

"Especially if you let them walk right through you. Right, Jonah?" Eliza said, smirking.

Jonah ignored her, glancing at Henry. "She has a glow too. But it's not nearly as bright as ours."

"Yes, that's right," he said. "Every person is born with it. It's the essence of who they are, the image of God. It's Elohim's fingerprint—it comes from the soul. But when humans have chosen to ignore Elohim, to resist Him, they cannot experience the full life—and therefore the full light—that He wants them to have. They live as shadows of themselves. Their light is diminished. Like hers."

Jonah stepped off of the pathway and onto the green grass. All the buildings, cars, and streets looked exactly the same in the hidden realm. But there was a kind of electricity that ran over the grass he was standing on, subtle, but there. It appeared alive, and in a constant state of motion.

"Look at the grass!" Eliza said. "And the trees!"

The branches of the trees in the park had a pale, but similar, electrical glow.

"They're alive," Henry said, reaching up to hold a tree branch, which seemed to grow brighter when he touched it. "Anything Elohim creates has His mark all over it. Not a soul, like people do. But they do have His touch."

"Okay. So where's Mom?" Electric grass or not, Jonah was ready to find his mother. "Are there any other clues about where they are holding her?"

The natural smile faded from Henry's face, and he shoved his hands in his pockets. "Like I said before . . . we know she's in the hidden realm, but beyond that . . . we're not exactly sure."

Eliza took a step closer to him, arms folded. "Aren't you supposed to know what's going on here?"

"I'm a guardian angel," Henry said. "I'm here because it's my duty to protect you as much as I can. But I'm not a warrior-class angel. Not yet." Jonah thought there was an edge of disappointment in his voice.

Eliza rolled her eyes and turned her back toward Henry. Henry was staring down at the asphalt pathway beneath his feet, clearly ashamed he didn't know more.

"While we're trying to figure out what to do, you could at least give us a few pointers," Jonah said helpfully. "We haven't had a lot of practice with these new abilities and we could really use some help before we get attacked again."

Henry perked up a little. "Good idea, Jonah."

He motioned them to stand in the middle of the grassy field.

"Jonah, you start with your arrows. Fire them at the fire hydrant over there."

Jonah reached back over his shoulder, and, just like it had in the alleyway, an arrow appeared in his right hand, a bow in his left.

"Good!" Henry said. "Now aim and fire."

"But what if I hit it?" Jonah said uneasily. "I don't want to destroy it and blast water all over the place or anything . . . well, okay, maybe that would be awesome, but I'd rather not wreak any unnecessary havoc right this moment."

"If we were back in the physical world, then, yes, that would be a concern," Henry said. "But in the hidden realm, your arrows don't harm objects that aren't alive. They have no concern for them. This is a spiritual world, remember? Angel arrows can only harm spiritual beings."

His voice darkened. "Just make sure you don't ever get hit by one. Humans are spiritual. If you get hit, it doesn't just hurt a little bit. You die. And I wouldn't want that to happen on my watch."

Jonah raised his eyebrows at Henry, then turned back to

his target. He aimed at the fire hydrant and released. The arrow flew lazily off to the right, fizzling when it hit the side of the building.

"Eliza," Henry said, "go ahead and see if you can form a shield."

He stood behind Jonah, repositioning his legs, back, and arms into a better stance, and giving him a few more pointers. Jonah shot a few more, each one getting better.

Eliza had extended her hands above her head and formed the shield.

Henry smiled. "That's great, Eliza! The shield of faith. Excellent. Now, here's what you need to know. The stronger your faith is, the stronger the shield becomes."

The light of her shield grew fainter. Her hands stayed raised, but she looked at him uncertainly. "To tell you the truth, faith is not something I've been very good at, Henry."

"Don't worry," he said. "It's obviously stronger than you think it is. It is called a shield of *faith*, you know. You have to have some to be able to form it." She breathed a little easier as he said this, and the light of the shield grew stronger again.

"Good! Now, the key to a strong shield is this—close your eyes, and rid your mind of everything. Everything that bothers you, that you worry about, even that you feel. And let your mind focus on Elohim, and Him alone. Imagine what He looks like, what He sounds like. Picture Him right there beside you."

Henry raised his hands above his head and immediately produced a shield of bright golden light that went all the way around him, so bright that Eliza had to cover her eyes. He quickly extinguished it.

"See?"

She nodded obediently and tried again, squinting her eyes

shut. After a minute, she opened one eye. Her shield wasn't any brighter. In fact, it may have grown slightly weaker again.

Eliza dropped her arms in frustration, and the shield disappeared.

"It will happen," Henry said. "It just takes time. And practice." He turned toward Jonah again, and Jonah couldn't help but see the lack of confidence on Eliza's face. Faith was hard. They'd never felt until today, though, like their lives depended on it.

Jonah's aim was getting a little better each time. He shot two more arrows that narrowly missed their mark. The third one hit the fire hydrant squarely in the center. Jonah pumped his fist in the air and Henry cheered.

"Nice shot," said Eliza.

As Jonah pulled another arrow and Henry and Eliza looked on, a man in a business suit carrying a briefcase came around the corner of a nearby building, walking along the street across the lawn. They saw a very dim glow in the center of his chest, no brighter than if he were holding a lit match in front of him. Over his shoulder sat a black, winged creature. It had its gnarled claws dug into the man's back, and it was busily whispering in his ear. The creature was so focused, he didn't notice the three pairs of eyes watching him.

The creature made Jonah's heart pound. He brashly leveled the arrow at him and prepared to release.

Henry grabbed the shaft of the arrow before Jonah could let it go. The bow and arrow disintegrated in Jonah's hands.

"Not now," he said calmly. "You need to stay focused on getting your mom back. He didn't see us, and I'd like to keep it that way. The less fallen angels know about you, the better your chances."

Jonah didn't like seeing the fallen one with his claws in that man's back, but Henry was right. They needed to concentrate on the mission in front of them.

"I wonder how long that creature has been on that man's back," Eliza said, concern in her voice.

"It could be mere days," said Henry. "Or years. Judging by how dim he was, I'd say a very long time."

"But doesn't he know?" Jonah asked. "How could you not be aware that a fallen angel is on your back?"

Henry smiled sadly. "They are crafty creatures, the Fallen. They start with a whisper, an encouragement. Pushing him toward self-absorption. Telling him he doesn't need anyone. Soon he's telling him he doesn't even need Elohim. Before the man knows it, the creature has his claws in him and won't let go."

Jonah shivered as the man rounded the corner, the fallen angel digging in deeply, and walked back into the shadows.

"So what do we do now?" Eliza asked. To their backs was the Hudson River and to the right, a subway station. In front of them were three streets heading in different directions.

"For we walk by faith, not by sight," Henry murmured.

Eliza looked up at him. "Isn't that from the Bible?"

"Yes. Second Corinthians 5:7," he said as he studied the roads in front of them. "It's how we are going to find Eleanor. Trust that Elohim is going to show us the way."

Jonah frowned. "Sounds kind of low-tech, don't you think? Isn't there something a little more advanced than just *faith*? Isn't that what this watch is for?"

He held it up and pushed the button again. Nothing happened. The old watch hands read 5:58.

"The MissionFinder 3000 won't work here in the hidden

realm," Henry answered. "Lean into your faith. It's more power-ful than you realize. Especially when it's all you have."

As they stood contemplating their choice of directions, try-ing to figure out how to "walk by faith," something rustled behind a row of bushes.

"Did you hear that?" Eliza said.

Before anyone could answer, they heard the sound of some-thing moving across the concrete. They followed the noise until it stopped behind the small building that held the entrance to the subway.

Henry stood very still, watching for even the tiniest move-ment. Finally, he began walking silently toward it.

Creeping around the other side of the building, he flapped his wings once, and suddenly disappeared behind it in a blur of energy.

"Aha!" Jonah and Eliza heard him say. Grunts and a few high-pitched growls were all they heard for a few seconds, but Henry finally emerged.

And he was not alone.

He was dragging a long, greenish creature with him.

"Look what I found!" he said, breathing heavily and holding the animal up in front of them.

Both Jonah and Eliza took a step back.

"It's a snake!" Eliza said, crinkling up her nose.

Henry held it just below its head. It was at least six feet long, its body thrashing back and forth. But the angel held it tightly in his grip, far enough away that it couldn't reach him. It was the greenish-brown color of a slimy pond.

Its mouth was open, showing two razor-sharp fangs, trying to get at Henry's hand. Its tongue was slithering around frantically.

At the same time that it was trying to bite the angel, it spat and made screeching noises, almost as if it were speaking another language.

It was the eyes, though, that Jonah was drawn to the most. Piercing yellow, like the other fallen ones he had seen. They strained and glared at him. And he was sure that if looks could kill, not one of them would be standing here right now.

FIFTEEN

THE BRIDGE TO BROOKLYN

Henry seemed slightly surprised that he'd actually caught this creature, but he held it up higher and said, "Silence!" This only made it scream louder, however.

"Fine, have it your way." Henry drew his arm back and made a throwing motion toward its mouth. Glowing cords appeared in the air, wrapping around its snout. He held on to the creature with both hands so it wouldn't slither away. Finally it stopped flailing around so much.

"There are snakes in the hidden realm?" Jonah said.

Henry nodded. "The hidden realm is full of mysterious creatures. I've never actually seen one of these guys this close. My guess is it was watching us and getting ready to report back to its superiors."

Jonah didn't want to think about what that would mean.

"You mean it can talk?" Eliza asked.

"Oh yes," said Henry. "Those screeches you heard? That was its native tongue."

"Well, it's a good thing you caught it, then, Henry," Jonah

said, leaning over a little closer to study the creature. "Maybe it knows where they're holding Mom and the others."

The snake glared at him as he spoke, as if it knew exactly what he was saying. Its mouth remained closed but it growled, like it was daring them to try to get anything out of it.

"Do you think it can understand us?" Eliza asked, noticing how it had appeared to listen to Jonah's words.

"Let's find out," Henry said, turning to face the creature again. "Do you know what I am saying? Can you understand me?"

The snake looked away from him and exhaled heavily out of its nose, wriggled again unsuccessfully, and finally nodded.

"Excellent," said Henry. "If I take the chains off your mouth, will you be quiet?"

It gave an abrupt nod again, and Henry reached toward its mouth.

"Hold on a second!" Eliza said. "Do you really believe that it won't just start screeching again? Or try to bite us?"

"Only one way to find out." Henry gave the glowing chains a tug. They disappeared in a puff of white smoke.

"Can you speak to us? What is your name, snake?"

"I am a serpent," a high-pitched voice hissed back at the angel. "There is a difference. My name is Salmir. I have lived on the Lower Island for many centuries. And you three, by your very presence here . . . *are in danger.*" He seemed to almost grin as he hissed again, if snakes could really do that.

Jonah smirked. "We're the ones who have caught you. Looks like you're the one in danger here."

Salmir sneered at him, burying the gaze of his yellow eyes in Jonah. "Boy, what are you doing in a place like this? Shouldn't you be at home in your crib, all safe and sound?"

Henry spoke firmly. "I will need to put your muzzle back on if you continue to be rude, snake."

"Of course, my dear *guardian* angel. How thoughtless of me," the snake hissed sarcastically. "How can I be of service to you and your *powerful army* today?" He grinned, showing his two sharp fangs.

"Do you know where the nephilim are?" demanded Jonah. He strung an arrow from his back and stepped forward. "Have you seen them? Tell us where they are, or I swear I'll—"

"No need to get angry, sir," Salmir said, a suddenly submissive tone in his voice as his eyes followed the tip of the arrow. "Salmir is at your service. You seek the nephilim? Yes, I may have heard of one or two nearby. Very rare creatures they are. Very powerful."

"Keep it aimed at him, Jonah," said Henry. "If he can lead us to the nephilim, we can have your mom back in no time at all." Jonah kept the white-tipped arrow trained on the serpent.

Eliza still had her arms crossed, glaring at the creature. "He'll just take us right into a trap. You guys don't honestly think that this servant of Abaddon is going to help us, do you?"

"I am no servant of Abaddon," Salmir hissed again. "Salmir is the servant of no one, neither man nor angel!"

"And we're supposed to believe that?" Eliza muttered.

Henry raised his eyebrows at Jonah and Eliza.

"Right now," Jonah said, his eyes not leaving the snake, "this . . . serpent . . . is our best bet. If he's seen a nephilim and knows where they are, he can lead us there."

"Or else run the risk of being turned into black dust," Henry said sternly.

"Yes, yes," Salmir said. "I will take you where you want to go.

And then you will release me. If you don't find what you are looking for, I am your servant forever."

"Ewww," Eliza said, disgusted. "Who would want a slimy snake for a servant?"

"But"—he glared at her—"I will need to be let go if I am to be of assistance."

Jonah nodded at Henry. It was decided.

"Okay, we'll take your deal," Jonah said, as Henry dropped him to the ground, pulling an arrow off his own back and aiming it at Salmir too.

"But I am warning you," said Jonah. "If you try anything, or lead us down the wrong path, you will have to answer to Elohim Himself."

Upon hearing that name, Salmir winced, as if he were in extreme pain.

"Don't say that!" he screeched. "That name. I can't stand it!"

They watched him writhe in pain for a few seconds before he finally settled down.

"The Bible says there is power in His name," Henry said as he studied Salmir. "Some of the Fallen can't stand for His name to be said. That seems to be the case with this creature too."

"Maybe that's how we can control him," Jonah said.

"Or maybe it's proof that we shouldn't trust him. If he really didn't serve Abaddon, then Elohim's name wouldn't bother him," Eliza argued.

The serpent winced, but said nothing.

"That's a risk we're going to have to take," Jonah said grimly, eyeing the serpent.

"We have a journey ahead of us, my new friends," Salmir said. "These streets lead to many mystifying places. Places full of shadows, where you might stumble upon something you'd rather not see." He hissed a laugh, then suppressed it. "What I mean is, you certainly need a guide, and you have chosen the right one to take you where you need to go."

Henry floated up above them, his arrow still aimed at the serpent's head. Jonah followed behind, taking careful aim as well. Salmir slithered toward the three streets in front of them and chose the third one. A dim streetlight flickered against gray buildings. It was still mostly dark, even though the sun was on its way up.

"Down this road," Salmir said in a high quiver, eyeing the arrows. "Come, follow me. I'll take you to the nephilim."

He slithered ahead, followed by Henry, and then Jonah and Eliza. Jonah was growing more and more anxious by the minute to see his mother.

Eliza fell behind a little, trudging after them.

"Hurry up, Eliza!" Jonah called.

"I'm walking as fast as I can," she replied. "But I have to tell you, I don't like this. How do you know he's going to lead us to Mom and not into more trouble?"

"We have him right where we want him. And honestly, we don't have another option right now," said Jonah. "Just think about finding Mom and getting out of here as fast as we can."

Salmir slid ahead, making rights and lefts around buildings, passing by, and sometimes through, humans, who continued on their way, unaware of any unseen presence. So far, he was living up to his word. He wasn't trying to run away. He watched their arrows carefully. Every so often he would slow down, beckoning them on farther.

"Come on, come on, angel, and my human friends," he would hiss. "Right this way. Hurry up."

Soon a massive bridge came into view. It was made from stone and steel, with thousands of cables running from the base to the peaks at the two center supports. Lights that sparkled like stars ran along it, covering a mile of water, from Manhattan to Brooklyn. The Brooklyn Bridge.

"That's the biggest thing I've ever seen," Eliza said, in awe.

There was a wooden walking path down the middle of the upper level of the bridge, while cars and trucks drove beneath it. Walkers and bikers were moving along the walkway in both directions, but none were aware of what was happening in the hidden realm. Salmir slithered his long body up on the path, calling them to follow.

Eliza stopped and pointed to the end of the bridge. "Are you telling us that the nephilim are in Brooklyn?"

"Yes, yes," Salmir said, almost gleefully. "Come, my friends. Our journey takes us this way. Hurry along now."

He slinked down the walkway across the bridge. Jonah looked at Henry, who suddenly began to look uncertain.

"Well," Jonah said to them both, "what choice do we have? Let's go across the bridge."

Henry seemed about to protest, but stopped. Jonah stepped onto the walkway with Eliza one step behind him. Henry followed, a wrinkle of worry still on his forehead.

Cars raced below their feet as they moved along the bridge. Jonah kept his eyes and arrow trained on Salmir, slithering quickly ahead of them.

"Come along," he called out again. "We must cross this bridge. Your nephilim lies not far away. We're very close now."

"I don't like this," Eliza muttered to Jonah as they walked. "Not one bit. We're following a snake across the Brooklyn Bridge.

And we have no idea what's on the other side, waiting for us. It's insane!"

"I know, Eliza, it seems kind of crazy," Jonah admitted. "But what other choice do we have? We don't know our way around down here, and he does. Sometimes you just have to trust."

They were almost at the middle of the bridge now, and every few seconds Salmir continued to coax them on.

"Hurry up, friends," he hissed. "Don't want to be late to find Mommy, do we?"

Jonah continued moving, but with each step, he began to sense that maybe Eliza was right. Holding on to the railing, he looked down into the traffic below and started to feel queasy.

They were almost halfway across when Salmir glanced back at them again, yellow eyes narrowing. Jonah thought he saw him flash an evil grin, and suddenly he began to slither, much faster than before, toward the end of the bridge.

"Hey! Where are you going?" Jonah yelled. But within seconds, he had slid off the end of the bridge, disappearing down a side street. Jonah didn't even have time to fire an arrow at him.

"What is he doing? Where did he go?" Eliza shouted, but no sooner had she said the words than Jonah heard a scraping sound behind them.

He looked back for Henry.

But Henry was gone.

"Henry?" he called out, searching the sky. Maybe he had flown up to get a better view of Salmir. At the same time, he heard a large splashing sound in the waters below. They looked down at the water and saw nothing but swirling water and bubbles.

"Henry!" Eliza screamed, leaning over the edge of the walkway.

They were quiet, listening. But all they could hear was the traffic passing below.

"Did he just . . . jump in the river?" asked Jonah, watching the bubbles. Before Eliza could try to answer, a long black tentacle shot up out of the water.

Jonah pulled her away from the edge of the bridge, which caused both of them to fall down in the middle of the path. The tentacle grabbed at the air where they had been standing, and instead latched onto a large steel cable.

"J-J-Jonah," Eliza stammered. "What is that?"

"I don't know," he cried out as he pushed himself up off the ground and pulled Eliza to her feet. "But whatever it is, I'm guessing that's what took Henry!"

A young woman on a bicycle rode past them, enjoying the view of the city, totally oblivious to the fact that a giant tentacle was holding on to the Brooklyn Bridge.

Another tentacle shot up out of the water, sending Jonah and Eliza shuffling backward. It grabbed another steel cable, wrapping itself around. The two tentacles were thicker than Volkswagens. Jonah wondered how big the creature that the tentacles were attached to was.

He didn't have to wait long to find out. With its two arms grasping the cables, the monster began pulling itself up.

A mouth full of teeth emerged first, each one bigger than Jonah. There must have been hundreds. The creature had ten tentacles, a long, snakelike body, and a thrashing tail covered with razor-sharp spikes. Red eyes glared at them as it whipped its head back and forth viciously. Three other tentacles had grabbed the bridge as the monster pulled. Another stretched out over the water, away from them, holding an angel.

"Henry!" Eliza shouted. He was water-drenched and dazed, trying to find his bearings. The creature held its captive out for them to see, as if it were taunting them.

Jonah pulled a white arrow off his back and tried to steady his shaking hands. The monster saw the gleam of the arrow and growled angrily, bearing down on him. Aiming at the tentacle that held Henry, he took a deep breath and let it fly. The arrow soared over Henry's head and past the monster, floating down into the water below.

Quickly Jonah pulled another arrow, aimed again, and fired. This time it hit the tentacle squarely. But it bounced off, landing harmlessly in the water. Shakily he fired another. His aim was true, but the arrow might as well have been a feather for all the damage it did.

"It has armor, Jonah!" Henry shouted. "It's impenetrable. Your arrows are just making it angrier!"

The creature reared its head back, and a blast of fire came from its mouth and nostrils and shot a hundred feet up in the air. A wave of heat hit Jonah like he was standing in front of an open furnace.

This thing can breathe fire? They had definitely ticked the sea monster off.

Jonah peeked up again, long enough to see it shoot flames into the air a second time. He rolled himself over behind a stone column and swallowed hard. Glancing over to his left, he saw Eliza crouching behind another part of the bridge, doing her best to hide herself. They both heard Henry's cries as he was thrashed back and forth through the air.

"Eliza!" Jonah called out. But she was too busy staring at the monster to hear him. She was watching it intently, like she was almost studying it. The monster leaned its head back and blew fire out of its mouth a third time. Amazingly, Henry thought he saw a slight smile curve on Eliza's lips.

The monster reared back and roared so loudly that Jonah and Eliza had to cover their ears. It snapped its spiky tail quickly and pulled hard with its tentacles, propelling its massive body onto the bridge, Henry still held captive in one of its tentacles. Before Jonah could call out to Eliza, he saw her stand up.

And then she walked out in the middle of the bridge directly in front of the monster.

"Eliza!" Jonah shouted. "Get down! What are you doing?"

She ignored him, eyes squarely on the beast. Its red eyes found her and narrowed, focusing on its prey.

In a split second, it dawned on Jonah. *She wants to be seen!*

Satisfied that the creature had targeted her, Eliza began to retreat down the bridge, walking backward. When she saw it begin to follow her, pulling itself along the bridge, she began to run.

"I'm going to need your help, Jonah!" she called out to him.

The monster seemed to be infuriated by this little girl in front of it. Picking its head up, it opened its huge jaws, exposing gigantic teeth and the blackness of its slimy throat. Smoke swirled around its tongue.

It cocked its head back to breathe fire again, and when Eliza saw that, she hit the ground.

A blast of flames shot across the bridge.

Jonah stood up and held his breath. The creature was past him now, and in all of the smoke and flames, he couldn't see his sister anywhere.

Then a figure stood up on the bridge. Eliza! Running again. Jonah looked ahead of her and realized where she was headed.

Two giant stone towers upheld the massive bridge. She was going for the first one, as fast as she could. Eliza was no longer turning around to make sure the monster followed. Now she was in an all-out sprint.

Jonah chased them both. The creature moved fast and was gaining on her. Jonah felt his feet transform again, and he surged forward. But even with the angel-power of his shoes, he could tell he would never get there in time. The beast was moving too fast.

Eliza was determined, though. Jonah watched as she continued to run as fast as she could. The monster charged ahead furiously, a tentacle reaching out, just behind her foot.

But she was through the opening in the stone tower.

And the beast was unable to stop.

It crashed through the opening, but its enormous body could not fit. Only its head and neck extended through Eliza's side of the tower. The rest of its body thrashed around, but was hopelessly wedged inside the stone structure.

Jonah quickly made his way through the other side of the opening, which was clear, narrowly avoiding the swinging tentacles of the frustrated monster.

Eliza stood to the side with her hands on her knees, breathing deeply, but smiling at Jonah.

He wanted to yell at her, but there was no time. They still had to deal with this creature and try to save Henry.

"Come with me!" she said, and she bounded up on the creature's back.

"Eliza!" Jonah yelled. "Seriously?"

But she wasn't listening. He breathed in deep and followed her onto the beast.

It began to twist its head fiercely, aware of the kids on its back.

"Whoa!" Jonah said, as he stumbled and almost fell, barely able to grab onto a thick plate of armor. Eliza was just ahead of him.

"Come on!" she shouted. "We need to get on top!"

"Why?" he yelled. "What are we doing?"

She rolled her eyes and motioned urgently. "No time to explain. Just come. Now!"

He hopped up beside her, and they were clinging to the monster's neck just as it reared back again to blast the sky with another round of fire from its gut.

"Pull an arrow!" she commanded. Jonah did as he was told.

And then he realized what Eliza had seen down on the bridge a few minutes ago. He knew why she had brought them here. As the creature pulled its head back to breathe its fire, for the slightest second, the scales of armor around its neck loosened. Eliza grabbed one of the scales and pulled it back. Underneath was soft, pink flesh.

Jonah knew what he had to do. He aimed the arrow down and let it go. It buried itself deep in the monster's skin and disappeared.

The next few seconds moved in slow motion. They quickly jumped off, as the creature reeled its head back and wailed in pain. From its mouth came an awful gurgling sound, and it somehow pulled itself back through the opening. Floundering around on the bridge like a beached fish, it finally flopped over the edge. They heard a huge splash in the water below, and then nothing but silence.

Jonah looked at Eliza as they panted and dusted themselves off. She was busy cleaning and straightening her glasses.

"Good thinking, Eliza," he said gratefully. "You're crazy, though."

"Thanks," she said, and hugged him tightly around the neck.

"Okay, okay," he said, blushing. "Let's see if we can find Henry."

They hurried over to the edge of the bridge and peered over. All they could see were white bubbles.

"Henry!"

Jonah's voice was unanswered.

Eliza screamed down at the water. "Henry!"

They watched, waiting for the angel to hurtle out of the river, a silver flash in the pale morning light.

No movement. The waters were still again.

Sitting down on the cold asphalt, neither spoke for a few minutes.

"Do you think he's . . . ?" Eliza couldn't finish her sentence.

"Angels can't die, remember?" said Jonah. "He has to be . . . somewhere." But he had no idea where.

"What was that thing?"

Eliza thought for a second. "A leviathan, if I'm not mistaken. It was a sea monster written about in the Psalms, and I think the book of Job. It was a creature created by Elohim, and there was a day when it ruled the sea."

"Those creatures are still around today?"

Eliza shrugged her shoulders. "Think about it. We've been under attack by a pack of wild cougars, a talking snake, and now the leviathan. It looks like Abaddon can make these animals do what he wants them to do."

"I'm not sure anyone could make that thing do what he wanted," said Jonah. "But I'll say this—Salmir knew exactly what he was doing."

Eliza threw a pebble across the bridge and watched as two

teenagers on mountain bikes crossed in front of her. They had no idea.

"I don't want to be the know-it-all sister here," she said quietly. "But I told you it was a bad idea to follow that snake. He led us onto this bridge, where we almost got killed by a biblical sea creature, and who knows how many other monsters are out there. And we aren't one step closer to finding Mom." She tried to control it, but her voice cracked with emotion.

Jonah sighed. She was right. They weren't any closer to finding their mother. And now Henry was gone, and he was their only guide in the hidden realm. Jonah was on the verge of despair himself. If they couldn't pull together, then there was no way they were going to be able to rescue their mother.

The words of their guardian angel flooded his mind. "Remember what Henry said back there? That we are to walk by faith, not by sight?"

She brushed a hot tear from her eye with her sleeve. "Yeah. So?"

"Well, maybe if that's going to happen, we actually ought to, you know, ask Elohim," he said. He had never been one to pray out loud with other people, not his sister, or anyone else. But right now, it seemed like the right thing to do.

Actually, it seemed like the *only* thing to do at the moment.

Eliza nodded and they bowed their heads just as the sun peeked through the clouds over the New York City skyline.

SIXTEEN

JONAH'S VISION

Immediately words began forming in Jonah's mind, almost as if the inside of his eyelids were a movie screen that he was viewing. Words from a passage of Scripture that he had learned long ago in Sunday school filled his mind.

For I am convinced that neither death nor life, neither angels nor demons, neither the present nor the future, nor any powers, neither height nor depth, nor anything else in all creation, will be able to separate us from the love of God that is in Christ Jesus our Lord.

The words were like ice pouring into the boiling waters of his thoughts. Nothing could come between him and Elohim. Even here, with evil enemies at every turn, they were inseparable.

As quickly as the words had appeared, they fell away, but they were replaced by another image that flickered to life. It was as if he were looking through a skylight.

He was peering down from the ceiling of a room with a dirty concrete floor and tile walls. All the way around it were people lying in hospital beds, tied down with leather straps, then covered with some sort of electrical shield that reminded him of the one that Eliza could create. There were seven in all, and one last bed sat empty, as if reserved for another unlucky prisoner.

The Fallen were everywhere, some standing in front of the nephilim, on guard. Others congregated in the middle of the room in small groupings. The guards held spearlike weapons and sneered at their captives. The others paced, as if they were anticipating something. They all appeared to be waiting. *One of the nephilim must not have arrived yet,* Jonah thought.

Then the image drew closer to the captives, like a camera zooming in. He closed in on one particular nephilim, and his mother's face came into full view. Jonah's heart leapt into his throat. Her face was battered and bruised, a cut across her cheek. Her clothes were torn, and her wrists and legs were bleeding from the straps that held her against the bed. Judging by how she looked, she had apparently fought against the restraints for a while, but had finally given up. Her head was turned to the side, and in a panic he wondered if she was still alive. But as the image drew closer still, so that now he seemed to be floating just above her, he saw her head move and her eyelids flutter.

And then she looked up, right at him, with the same clear green eyes he had looked into every day of his life. For several seconds they stared at him, the eyes of his mother, and somehow, he felt that she could see him too. Eleanor held her gaze as long as she could, and then her head collapsed back onto the bed. Her eyes closed again.

"Mom!" he shouted. "Mom, it's Jonah! I'm right here!" He reached out to her, but he began to move backward. He felt a tug on his hand, and suddenly he was passing through a gray fog and couldn't see anyone. He tried with everything he had to reach out to her and grab her, but the tug pulled him away as the image in front of him disintegrated like dust.

Another scene flashed across his mind now. He was flying over an expanse of trees, ponds, open green fields, and pathways. Like a bird, he soared just over the treetops, landing in the middle of the largest grass lawn he'd ever seen. To his left, in the distance, he saw the outline of tall buildings. And directly ahead of him, the turret of a castle rose above outstretched branches. As quickly as he had landed in the field, however, this image also began to fade.

Within seconds, it was gone.

He felt a tug again, and he was hurtling backward.

A moment later he was back on the Brooklyn Bridge.

She's alive. Mom is still alive.

"Jonah!" Eliza's voice sounded like it was a football field away, but came rushing toward him quickly. "Jonah! Are you there? What happened? Are you okay?"

"Yeah, I think so," he said groggily. "That was weird." The vision reminded him of the dreams he'd been having lately. Except ten times more vivid. He rubbed his eyes and saw Eliza, visible again in the morning sunlight, looking more like their mother than he'd ever noticed.

"I saw Mom."

Eliza leaned in closer to Jonah. "You *saw* her?"

"As clearly as I see you," Jonah answered. "I closed my eyes to pray, and suddenly it was like I was . . . transported to where she is, right now."

"Like a daydream, or something?" Eliza said, raising her eyebrows.

Jonah answered a little more harshly than he wanted. "No, I

was not daydreaming! I saw her, and it was really her! Not some part of my imagination going wild."

"Okay, okay," she said, backing down. "Just tell me everything you saw."

Jonah told her all he could remember, down to every last detail about the condition of his mother, the room, and the other nephilim. He described the Fallen, how many there were and what they were doing.

Eliza focused on him intently. "If what you saw is accurate, not just a daydream—"

"It's accurate," Jonah interjected. "I know it is."

"—then maybe it means we still have time," she continued. "It sounds like all of the nephilim, including Mom, are still alive, and waiting for the eighth and final one to arrive."

"I saw something else," Jonah said, closing his eyes tightly to try and remember all the details. "I was flying over a park, with trees and ponds. Then I landed in a huge field. I saw some really tall buildings in the distance. And then what looked like a . . . castle."

They thought about what this could mean for a minute. Eliza suddenly snapped her fingers.

"It's a park, with skyscrapers in the distance!" she said. "Don't you see? This is a clue. We know where we need to go next!"

Jonah stared at her blankly.

"Come on," she said, jumping up and patting the smoke out of her jeans. "A huge park, in the city—"

"Central Park!" Of course.

It actually seemed to make sense. Except for the castle part, which neither of them had an answer for. But that didn't matter right now. They were reenergized by Jonah's vision, and they bounded off the bridge and back toward Manhattan. If he was right, then their mom was still alive, and they had time. Renewed hope and strength fueled their footsteps.

"Henry's not here, so I guess we're riding the subway," Jonah said as they stepped onto the pavement.

Eliza remembered the weaving rocket ride he had taken them on earlier. "I wouldn't ride with him again anyway," she said. "But, Jonah, I hope he's okay. Wherever he is."

They found a subway station the next block over and descended underground. A dozen people were waiting for the next train.

They both stood and pondered the subway map for a few minutes. It was a spiderweb of lines, colors, and dots.

"It looks like to get to Central Park, we need to take this line here, then make a switch here." Eliza pointed at the map as she spoke.

The train echoed through the black cavern and finally screeched to a halt in front of them. Jonah hopped on, but not before two people walked right through him. Each time he felt a burst of electricity run through his chest. Each of them gasped and paused for a second before they kept walking.

"I don't think I'm ever going to get used to that," he muttered.

The car was almost half-full, and they stood at the back, against the wall. Jonah noticed that most of the passengers had a soft flicker of light coming from their chests—what Henry had called the image of God. A few looked more like Jonah and Eliza, a brighter light extending out to their fingertips.

The ones who have trusted in Elohim and accepted His love into their lives, Jonah thought. He was still amazed to see how evident it was here in the hidden realm. How real it all was.

The train made three stops before it was their turn to exit. They walked out of the train and into another underground station in order to make the transfer to one that ran north to Central Park. An express train bound for Grand Central Station came and picked up the waiting passengers, until they were the only ones left inside the cavernous waiting area.

A chill blew through the empty tunnel. "It sure is quiet in here," said Eliza, suddenly shivering.

"Yeah, and spooky too," Jonah said, listening for the next train.

He was peering down the tracks and into the dark tunnel when he heard a pattering sound. He watched as a rat appeared, scampering out of the tunnel.

"Wonder where that little guy is running to so fast?" Eliza said.

Another one followed him, and then three more. They scattered in all different directions, trying to find a crack to crawl in.

"I might not be a rat expert, but I don't think they're running *toward* anything," Jonah said. "They look like they're running *away* from something."

Just then, a group of at least a hundred rats poured out of the subway tunnel, climbing on top of each other, trying desperately to scale the walls. They disappeared down the other tunnel.

"That's strange behavior for rats, don't you think?" she said.

Something else was moving in the tunnel behind them, slowly clacking along. Eliza glanced at Jonah, who shifted uneasily.

Clack. Clack. Clack.

Jonah froze. "That sounds like—"

"—a cane." Eliza was thinking the same thing.

And then a pink-flowered dress came into view, a hunched-over old woman walking down the middle of the track, coming out of the tunnel.

"Can I get another hand with this map, dearies?" Her frail

voice echoed through the station, and high-pitched laughter split their ears.

"Run!" Jonah said. He turned, pulling Eliza with him, and sprinted toward one of the large concrete columns in the middle of the station. Something whizzed by his head and thudded above them, and the ceiling burst into flames. He dove to the ground and rolled behind the column, dragging Eliza with him. Looking up, they saw the black arrow that had knifed halfway into the rock disintegrate into dust.

Thud! Thud! Thud!

Three more arrows hit the column.

"She's back!" Eliza whispered desperately. "It's the same lady from the train!"

"And it looks like she brought some friends."

Jonah peeked around the corner in time to see her stand up straight, brandishing her cane, which was now a sword, in the air. He watched as she morphed into a tall, black-winged fallen angel. A half-dozen others were right behind her, all of them holding bows with flaming red arrows. Two fired, and Jonah whipped his head back as they narrowly missed the center of his forehead.

He remembered Henry's words. *"If you get hit, it doesn't just hurt a little bit. You die."*

Jonah breathed in heavily. Even though the Fallen were approaching, he couldn't shake the image of his mother, tied down to that hospital bed, no one there to help her. He gritted his teeth.

"Come on, Eliza," he said, crouching low and drawing a white-tipped arrow. "We can't let them do this. Not when we're this close to finding Mom!"

Wild-eyed, he turned and fired. As soon as he released the arrow, he reached back and pulled another, and then another. His arrows met two targets, piercing one of the Fallen through the neck, another in the chest. Gurgling screams filled the station as they fell.

The fallen ones were being directed by their leader, the subway lady, and they stood with black snarls on their faces as they fired their flaming arrows. One of them threw a spear that slammed into the wall beside Jonah, hitting it with such force that he was blasted back onto the ground.

Suddenly Eliza stepped around the corner and threw her hands into the air. A shield formed in front of them just as two arrows aimed right at their chests arrived. They dropped harmlessly onto the ground.

"Good one, Eliza!" Jonah said, and continued firing his arrows as fast as he could. His aim was rapidly improving. He keyed in on one particularly large and ugly fallen one, but his first arrow sailed over his head. He saw his target grimace and fire his black arrow toward Jonah. He ducked out of instinct as the arrow screamed in his direction, but then saw it bounce off Eliza's shield. Taking aim again, he took a deep breath and let go. His white flaming arrow buried itself in the fallen one's forehead, and he collapsed backward on top of another one that had been successfully pierced already.

Two of the fallen ones held large spears, taking aim together at Eliza's shield. They released them at the same time, and they hit the shield with enough force that it pushed Eliza back and onto the ground. Her glasses flew off, bouncing along the concrete, and the shield disappeared.

Three of the Fallen remained, including the subway lady. They raised their black, crumpled wings and flapped twice, sailing quickly toward them. Subway Lady's yellow eyes bulged out of her scaly black face as she grinned fiercely, landing on the path right in front of them. Her sword gleamed as she waved it in their faces, the tip of it bloodred.

"Very impressive, my dears," she snarled. "You've come such a long way. Your mother would be so proud. Too bad you're not going to ever see her again."

Jonah and Eliza stepped back as the three Fallen walked toward them. Jonah backed into a trash can, and he picked it up and threw it at them as hard as he could. The old lady batted it away as if she were swatting a gnat.

She raised her sword at Eliza, who hadn't been able to find her glasses. Jonah was sure all Eliza could see was a big, dark shadow, and all she could feel was fear and defeat, not faith. Crouching down, Eliza shielded her face. Subway Lady was posing to strike, and Jonah pictured his sister taking her last breath right in front of him.

The fallen angel brought her blade crashing down.

"Eliza!" Jonah rushed forward to try to put himself between the blade and his sister. But just before he could cover her, Eliza threw up her hands one more time. Just in time for the flickering shield of faith to block the blow.

Jonah seized the only chance he knew he was going to get. He pulled two arrows at once off of his back and didn't even bother stringing them.

He threw them as hard as he could.

Each arrow found its target, piercing the chests of the two fallen ones on either side of Subway Lady.

"Your turn!" he said as he leveled one last arrow, strung it, and let it fly.

It met her chest, and she screeched in pain and fell to the ground.

All of them now lay sprawled across the subway station, motionless. Jonah and Eliza caught their breath and watched as the Fallen began to disintegrate into black dust.

Finally Jonah whispered, "You think they're . . . dead?"

"I don't think so," Eliza said, sitting up. "They are eternal beings, just like the angels. They can't die. They must just . . . relocate." Eliza's brow wrinkled. "Like when Jesus sent the demons out of the boy and into the herd of pigs."

Jonah remembered. "They had to do exactly what Jesus told them to do. They became bound under Elohim's command."

Jonah found Eliza's glasses and handed them to her. She rubbed them on her shirt, and they watched as the black dust blew down around the subway tracks.

"Nice shooting, Jonah," Eliza said. "You're getting good. Wish I had a bow and arrow myself."

"Thanks, E, but be careful what you wish for. How many times have you saved our lives today with that shield of yours? Look at the Miami Heat. They would be nowhere without a killer defense, right?"

She stared at him blankly.

"Well, that's what you are, sis," he said. "Our killer defense."

Eliza smiled faintly as the subway train swept into the station.

"Let's get out of here," Jonah said, still looking warily around. "I personally don't ever want to experience that again."

SEVENTEEN

THE CASTLE

They tried to calm down as they rode the subway north toward Central Park, but it was difficult.

"You don't think anything bad happened to Henry, do you?" Eliza said darkly. "I'm worried, Jonah. We need help. We have no clue what we're doing."

Almost everything inside of him agreed with her. They had no idea where they were going, really, or what they were going to do when they got there. It was blind faith that moved them forward, following what Jonah had seen in his vision. Henry was gone, and they were alone.

And yet . . .

This was their mission, not anyone else's. Whether or not it seemed impossible, this was the path Elohim had put them on. That was going to have to be enough for now.

The electronic voice announced, "Next stop, Fifty-Seventh Street," and they exited the subway, just south of Central Park.

They walked across the bustling street when the light changed, unseen by the dozens of people who crossed with them. Most of the people glowed dimly, just visible in the morning light; every once in a while, though, they saw someone shining brightly as they walked, lighting up the pavement.

A large, stone wall surrounded the park, and they walked along it until they found the entrance—a paved pathway winding into the woods. It felt strange to Jonah to one minute be on a busy downtown street, and the next to find himself in what seemed like an old forest. But when they took a few steps in, the sights and sounds of the city were only a memory.

Jonah stopped in the middle of the pathway and sighed.

"Where to now?" Eliza asked. He glanced back at her but didn't respond.

He looked at the outline of dark trees and bushes, and a couple of pathways splitting off in front of them. He tried to remember the vision, but how was he supposed to know if this was the right place? Doubt began to creep into his mind. Even if this was the right place, the park was enormous, bigger then the entire downtown of Peacefield. How could he possibly know where their mother was being held?

Breathe, Jonah. Breathe.

He closed his eyes, slowing his mind down and trying to picture the vision again. The trees, ponds, and lawn all came into view, as well as the castle.

The castle.

His eyes popped open and he looked down the path, both ways.

"What is it?" Eliza said. "You remember something?"

He didn't answer, his mind racing. He continued searching the path until he spotted it. A sign, near the entrance. He sprinted back and stood in front of the sign. It showed a detailed map of the park. He ran his finger over the map, studying it intently.

"Belvedere Castle!" He stuck his finger on a point near the center of the map. That had to be it.

"The image from your vision?" Eliza panted, having chased him back down the path.

Jonah nodded. He felt a new energy course through him. "This is it. It's the only castle on here. And I just have this feeling . . ."

It was hard to explain, but somehow he knew this was where they needed to go. One more look at the map and he was beckoning her after him down the path.

"Let's be careful," Eliza said as they walked along, looking up at the trees. "It feels kind of dark in here."

They walked in silence for the next ten minutes, carefully watching the woods, more than once jumping at the movement of squirrels in the leaves. Crossing a bridge over a pond, they heard only their own footsteps across the wood. No one was there. Jonah figured even New Yorkers were scared of some parts of Central Park. Probably afraid of getting mugged. *They have no idea that the real threat might be fallen angels. Talk about scary.*

They came to a small wooden sign that said THE RAMBLE. Behind it was a narrow dirt path that wound downward, deeper into the forest. The growth looked much thicker here.

"I hate to say it, but I think we have to go this way to the castle," said Jonah.

Eliza peered down the path. "Looks creepy."

He stepped onto the path, followed reluctantly by Eliza.

Briars pressed in on both sides, so that they could only walk in single file. It grew dark, the dense trees blocking out the sun as they worked their way down into the wild, overgrown area. The air grew cooler by the second. Twice Jonah thought he saw a pair of yellow eyes watching them from behind a tree. He was tense, his hands ready to pull an arrow at a moment's notice. He had the distinct feeling that they were being watched. But so far, no one was attacking.

"Something's in here with us," Eliza whispered from behind. Jonah silently agreed but said nothing and tried to move as fast as he could. He was sure that the map showed that this was the fastest way to the castle.

He shivered in the darkness. The cold seemed to seep into his skin and down into his bones. It felt like icy fingers had suddenly reached inside his body and were searching, probing. Looking for a place inside him to grab and hold on to. Glancing back, he saw Eliza's strained expression and knew she was feeling the same thing.

It felt like fear, but wrapped in a deep, blanketing sadness.

Jonah's heart grew heavy, as if any minute it might fall out of his chest and crack into a million frozen pieces. The fingers continued reaching inside him as he willed his legs to move, and the sadness turned into despair.

Despair quickly spiraled into hopelessness.

He felt himself slowing down, his limbs growing stiff and numb. *What's the point?* They were never going to find his mother. They couldn't possibly defeat the hordes of Abaddon. They were just a couple of kids. Their guardian angel was gone—forever, for all he knew.

What were we thinking?

Grief began icing over him. Misery moved in like an impenetrable fog, and he stopped moving. He sat down in the dirt and began to weep. Eliza dropped beside him and began sobbing too.

"There's so much . . . darkness," Jonah gasped.

Tears covered Eliza's face as she looked up. "I just . . . don't think I can . . . keep going, Jonah. I feel so . . . so . . ."

"Sad," whispered Jonah, head hanging between his knees.

"What is this place? Where are we?"

He didn't answer. He didn't know.

All Jonah could think, all he knew, was that they were totally and completely lost.

But then something stirred inside him. Somewhere deep inside, beneath the pain, below the sadness, in the small, tucked-away place the icy fingers had been grappling for but could not reach, his soul had whispered one solitary word. One desperate word, the last word of hope he knew.

Elohim.

The word fluttered gently at first, but grew stronger, working its way through the blanket of sadness covering his heart. It went up into his thoughts, and finally into his mouth.

"Elohim," he whispered, his voice barely audible.

Eliza stirred beside him, and Jonah heard her breath catch, followed by the rustle of leaves as she leaned into the dense under-growth to peer at something farther down the path, on the other side of Jonah.

"Jonah, look," she said with a tired voice.

It felt like his head was made of cold steel, but he finally forced his chin up off of his chest and looked.

Through the darkness, ahead of them on the path, he saw it.

A single dot of light.

They both stared at the glowing pinprick. It was pure and dazzling white. Jonah felt a tinge of warmth as he focused on it, which took an edge off the cold.

Jonah forced himself up slowly and finally stood. Grabbing

Eliza's hand, he helped pull her up beside him, and they steadied themselves for a few seconds.

"Keep looking at the light," he said. "Let's walk toward it."

"I . . . I don't think I can," said Eliza, sounding as if she might break down in tears again.

Words made their way to Jonah's mouth again. He forced his lips to form the words and speak them.

"Give her strength, Elohim. Give us strength."

They held on to each other and began to move, only inches at first. With each step, though, their strength began to come back. They were climbing up a slow incline, out of The Ramble, continuing to look at the light that was piercing the darkness around them. The blackness began to lose its grip; the cold wasn't so harsh anymore. Daylight began to envelop them again, and the shadows faded into the distance behind them.

Finally they came to a pond and walked up onto a bridge.

Jonah stood in the middle of the footbridge and breathed in deep, his head feeling clear now.

"You okay?" he asked Eliza.

She swallowed and nodded slowly. "I think so. I've never felt like that before. I just wanted to give up. On everything."

"Me too. That place was seriously evil." He shuddered, thinking about what would have happened if they hadn't had Elohim to rely on.

His eyes adjusted to the bright sunlight as he looked across the pond. Scanning the tops of the trees slowly, he noticed a column rising just above the tree line. A flag waved softly in the breeze.

"The castle!" he said, pointing toward the column. "The one I saw in my vision. That's it!"

They bounded down the pathway together, filled with new energy, and with a new batch of nerves. What was there? Would they find their mother, and would they be able to rescue her?

The small stone castle sat on the edge of another pond. It appeared to grow naturally out of the rocky ground. Jonah wondered why something like this would be in the middle of Central Park, but they didn't have time for a history lesson. He knew it held the key to finding his mother, and he was more than ready to get her and go home.

Hiding behind a bushy tree, Jonah and Eliza peered through the leaves at the castle entrance.

"What are we supposed to do? Just walk right in?" Eliza asked. "I don't see anyone there."

"It looks like that's the only way to get inside," Jonah said, watching the door. "And if what I saw in my vision was right, we have to get in there to find Mom."

He pulled the branches aside and was about to walk forward.

"Wait, Jonah!"

His foot was in midair when he froze. Eliza pointed toward the ground in front of them. Barely visible, a beam of red light shot across the ground, about a foot above the dirt. It extended in both directions, turning toward the back of the castle.

She picked up a handful of dirt and tossed it in the air. As the dust floated down, a web of beams appeared.

"Some kind of laser beams?" Jonah guessed as he pulled his foot back. They studied the beams for a few seconds.

"I don't know," said Eliza. "But I'm betting it's nothing we want to touch. Could be an alarm system, or they could even slice you to bits."

Jonah heard movement around the sides of the castle. "Shhh!"

he whispered, holding his hand up. Two large figures appeared, walking from opposite ends of the castle toward the door.

Easily eight feet tall, they walked in step with each other. They wore sand-colored body armor from head to toe, and helmets with face shields that made them look like futuristic robots. Both of the soldiers' eyes were covered by a dark visor, and even when the sunlight fell across the visors Jonah saw only flat blackness. He wondered if, behind those helmets, they had eyes at all.

But the only weapons these modern-looking warriors seemed to be carrying were long, jagged spears, which they gripped tightly in their hands as if they couldn't wait to run any intruder through.

Out of the corner of his eye, Jonah saw a flutter up above.

"Look!" he whispered. "Up in the tower!"

They could see at least four more soldiers, standing at attention in the tower, long spears in their hands. In between them, peering down, with hands shackled together, stood an angel who looked like a handsome teenage boy.

"Henry!" Eliza cried. Jonah put his hand on her arm and raised a finger to his lips. She lowered her voice to a gleeful whisper. "He looks like he's okay!"

"For now," Jonah replied. Those soldiers, whoever they were, were holding the guardian angel prisoner. But it was good to see his face, even here.

The door to the castle suddenly opened, and as the ghostly soldiers continued pacing, another figure stepped into the light. He wore a similar suit of armor and helmet, except his looked like black iron. The armor itself looked like it would weigh as much as the Stone family car. Instead of holding a spear, a long sword hung from his belt.

He slowly ambled between the guards, looked out into the

sky, and lifted off his helmet. Jonah and Eliza drew back, repulsed by what they saw. Skin hung from his cheekbones, but just barely. And in a few places, it had apparently fallen off, to expose muscle and bone. His scalp, hairless, was the same.

However, what was most disturbing to Jonah and Eliza were his eyes. Like two dark stones sunken into the ground, they had collapsed into their sockets. He muttered something to one of the soldiers. Jonah shivered as they watched from behind the tree.

"That guy looks like he's in charge," whispered Eliza. Jonah nodded.

"We have to get in there," he said. "We've got to help Henry. And this is where they are holding Mom!"

Eliza thought for a minute. "How are we supposed to get in there? The place is guarded by soldier zombies or whatever they are, and that's assuming we can get through these red beams of light somehow."

They both turned around and sat quietly in the grass. Jonah racked his brain. *How are we supposed to get into this castle? We can't just go straight through the door. So what do we do?* He grabbed a small stone in his hand and tossed it onto the ground in front of him in frustration. It tumbled down the hill.

"... *and the walls came tumblin' down ...*"

The lyrics to the old Sunday school song flooded his mind. His head snapped up and he turned around again to study the castle.

Could it really be that easy?

"Jericho," he said simply.

Eliza cocked her head. "What?"

"Jericho."

Jonah got up and dusted his hands off. "Stay here and don't come out until I tell you to. I'll be back in a minute."

"But—" she protested, but he wasn't listening. He stood with his eyes closed, concentrating. He prayed that Elohim would again give him the feet shod "with the preparation of the gospel of peace." Then his tennis shoes disappeared, replaced by the sandals.

"Sweet," he said. "Here goes nothing." And then Jonah began to run.

He focused on the edge of the red beams, staying just outside their reach. His feet began to move faster and faster. Running along the perimeter, he had to lean in a little to the left, he was moving so quickly.

In a blur, Jonah passed Eliza, standing there with her mouth open. One lap down.

Six more to go.

None of the soldiers had seen him during his first pass. He kept his head down, focusing on the ground in front of him. As he moved around again, he could tell that his feet were already beginning to wear a slight path out.

Two laps completed.

Jonah tried to move his legs even faster. On lap three, he felt the doubt creep in. *Is this really going to work? Maybe it's just an old story.*

He bore down, though, determined to push through the doubt. Four laps down, then five. He was a blur of energy, passing Eliza, who had apparently realized what he was up to and was quietly cheering him on.

It was on lap six that he felt the flat handle of the spear across his stomach. He went spinning into the air, did two flips, and landed on his back.

He uttered a low groan. The back of his head hurt, there was a gash across his left elbow, and his back throbbed. Slowly he opened his eyes. He saw towering trees above him, sparkling both with the light of the hidden realm and the sun breaking through. Then the shadow of a man covered it all up.

Jonah felt dizzy as the man stooped down over his face. Suddenly, he was looking into a pair of glaring, sunken eyes.

"Just who do we have here?" he said. "And what is it that you're doing, running around our little fortress? Awfully quick, for a mere child."

Jonah tried to sit up, but a gnarled, gruesome-looking hand shoved him back down to the dirt.

"Not so fast, boy. You haven't answered my questions."

Jonah craned his neck, looking for any sign of Eliza. He prayed that she had stayed hidden behind the tree.

"My name is Jonah," he said, and then coughed, spitting blood onto the ground. He had bitten his lip too.

"Nice to meet you, Jonah," the man said, yanking him to his feet. Jonah staggered, putting both hands on his knees. He noticed that he still had his sandals on. "Did you come for your friend Henry?"

Jonah picked his head up and looked into the decaying face.

"Oh yes, boy," he said. "You don't have to tell me who you are. I already know. Henry is your guardian angel. And one of those nephilim is your mother."

"You don't know anything about me," Jonah said, spitting again. He tugged against the grip on his arm, but it was solid. He glanced at his feet.

I just needed one more lap.

"You will come with me now," the man said, dragging Jonah along the path. "Abaddon will surely reward me handsomely for this capture."

Suddenly, a flash of white light erupted behind them. Something slammed into Jonah's back, pushing both him and his captor to the ground.

Eliza stood over them, her shield blazing! As she forced herself between Jonah and the soldier, Jonah realized that it must have been the soldier that crashed into him after receiving the impact of Eliza's erupting shield. Her shield brushed against Jonah's elbow now, its coolness actually soothing his aching cut.

"Go, Jonah!" she screamed. "One more lap! Go!"

The soldier grabbed his spear and slapped it across the shield. Eliza stumbled backward into the trees. He towered over her, spear raised, but she still had the shield around her.

Jonah hesitated. She could not hold off this monster for long. "Go!"

Hearing her voice again, he knew what he had to do. Jonah turned away from her and began to run again.

Elohim, I hope this works!

He sped around the corner, even faster than before. He heard the commander scream orders to his henchmen. A soldier jumped in front of him, spear raised.

Jonah closed his eyes and leaped. Somehow his speed carried him over the soldier's head, and he landed on the other side, and on his feet. He kept running. It wasn't much farther now, and all he could think about was what was happening to Eliza.

When he turned the last corner, he saw a group of soldiers standing in a line, spears thrust toward him, waiting. The commander was behind them, holding Eliza by the arm.

There was no time to stop. He was so close.

Jonah barreled at them full speed. When he was almost to the point of the first spear, he leapt again.

Everything slowed down in that moment. Jonah saw himself flying over the soldiers, watched their confused faces, and he heard Eliza scream. He landed flat on his stomach on the other side and glanced over toward the castle to see where he was.

Lap seven.

Jonah closed his eyes and waited for something to happen.

But nothing did.

He only felt the dull end of a spear planted forcefully on his back.

Great.

"Jonah!" Eliza was crying out to him. "Jonah!"

He turned his head to see her, the sister he had just let down. The sister he had just allowed to be captured, along with him.

"What?" he mumbled.

"There's one more thing," she said slyly, as the commander pulled him off of the ground. "Remember the story? I think we need to shout."

She was right. Jonah vaguely remembered that in the story of the battle of Jericho, Joshua and his troops shouted, claiming their victory before it happened.

Jonah and Eliza looked at each other. With one voice, they began to yell.

"Waaaaaaaaaaaaaaahhhhhhhhhhhhhooooooooooooooooooo!"

The commander sneered and tried to speak over the shouting. "Stop that! Shut your little mouths before I—"

But before he could finish, the ground started to rumble under their feet. Quietly at first, but quickly it grew stronger. Soon they couldn't even stand. Jonah, Eliza, and the soldiers were all sprawled out on the ground.

The castle shook violently. Jonah turned his head just in time to see the electrical webbing protecting the castle flicker, and then disappear entirely. The soldiers in the tower guarding Henry began falling over the edge and down onto the stone landing below. Two of them came tumbling out of the door as the ground continued to shake. Henry's chains had fallen off, and he flew up above the castle, hovering in the sky for a few seconds.

He spotted Jonah and Eliza and shot toward them like a bullet. Grabbing their outstretched hands, he pulled them over to a safer spot, fifty yards away from the tower.

It was not a moment too soon.

Cracks began to form in the dirt all around the castle and quickly turned into gaping holes. The ground was opening up everywhere, and the soldiers began to disappear, one by one. Everything continued to shake, and their commander dug his fingernails into the dirt around him. But it was not enough. He lost his grip and fell into the wide gap below him, deep down into the darkness.

All the soldiers were gone. Abruptly, the ground stopped shaking. Jonah, Eliza, and Henry watched as the giant cracks began to seal themselves up. Within seconds, the earth had healed itself, and everything was just as it had been.

Yet as violently as the castle had shaken, it was still standing.

"The walls didn't . . . you know . . . come tumblin' down," said Jonah.

Henry slapped him on the shoulder, grinning. "Remember, we are in the hidden realm, Jonah. The victory is not about bricks and stone coming down. It's a spiritual battle. Elohim, in His wisdom, has conquered our enemies."

EIGHTEEN

TUNNEL TO WARDS ISLAND

Brilliant!" Eliza said, hugging her brother, then, turning to Henry, "I didn't know if we'd ever see you again. When you went underwater with the leviathan and didn't come back up . . ."

"He wasn't letting go, no matter how hard I fought, that was for sure," said Henry. "There was a rumor among the angels after the great rebellion by Abaddon that he had figured out a way to control and command the leviathan. The only way it would release me is when the Fallen came for me. This must be some kind of holding tower that they use when they have a prisoner."

"And the soldiers?" asked Eliza.

"Philistines, and their leader, King Achish," Henry said. When her forehead wrinkled, he added, "Spirits, who used to be men, who warred against the people of Elohim in life. Now in death they are doing the same thing."

Eliza hugged herself tightly as she looked again at the ground the soldiers had been sucked into.

"Thank you, Jonah. Or maybe we should call you Joshua."

Henry smiled. "Just like when he led the people of Israel in the battle of Jericho. Very creative."

Jonah shrugged. "The song just kind of came to me. Somehow, I thought it might work."

They walked through the unguarded front doors of the castle and climbed the narrow staircase until they emerged outside, on top of the tower.

"So this is the place you saw in your vision, right?" asked Eliza.

Jonah looked out over the Great Lawn of Central Park and the surrounding woods. The city skyline rose high in the distance.

"This has to be it. There aren't any other castles in Central Park, are there?"

"Let's take a look around," Eliza suggested. "There must be clues around somewhere that can lead us to Mom."

They walked back down the steps, Jonah leading the charge. The main level was small. There was a long, wooden counter and a chair behind it. They inspected the room quietly for a few minutes and found nothing except another staircase, going down.

Jonah motioned for Eliza and Henry to follow him. They wound down the stairs and found themselves in a dark basement. Eliza located a light switch and flipped it. Fluorescent lights flickered on, illuminating desks, computers, and office furniture scattered all over the room. The floor was laid in stone, covered by a rug in the middle that had embroidered on it a picture of the castle, and the words THE HENRY LUCE NATURE OBSERVATORY.

"It looks like this place isn't a real castle," Eliza said, picking up a brochure from one of the desks. "It's actually a weather observation post."

"Whatever it is, I don't see any signs of Mom or the other

nephilim," Jonah said as he took a disappointed look around the room.

They wandered around for a few minutes, searching for any hints that would point them toward Eleanor Stone. Henry inspected the walls. Eliza shuffled through papers on the desks and tried to log on to the computers, which, of course, were password-protected.

Jonah stood in the middle, trying to think. *Where would they have taken her? Where could they possibly be?*

He sighed loudly, frustrated. Was this going to be another dead end, like the Brooklyn Bridge? He kicked irritably at the dirty rug he was standing on, and the edge peeled up. Underneath was more stone, but there was something else.

The rounded edge of a darker surface.

Jonah quickly pulled the rug off of the floor. He uncovered what appeared to be an ordinary manhole cover. But as he knelt down to take a closer look, he noticed subtle, strange markings all over the dark stone.

"Come look at this, guys," Jonah said as he ran his fingers over the raised images. They were pictures of snakes, the leviathan, and other strange creatures. Next to those were sneering carvings of the Fallen, some holding spears in the air, others spreading their wings fiercely or firing flaming arrows. There were pictures of horrible faces, mouths open like they were screaming.

What drew his eye most, though, was the face in the middle. It was larger than the rest, darkened by a black hood that covered his head. A swath of black hair came down across his left eye, but his right eye was visible, and bloodred. His cheekbones and chin seemed to almost push through his scarred skin. The corner of his mouth not covered by his hair was turned up in a vicious, toothy grin.

"Who is that?" Jonah asked Henry, pointing at the face.

"Pretty obvious, isn't it, Jonah?" he said gravely. "It is the Evil Lord, the Prince of Darkness. That image is of none other than Abaddon himself."

"Ew," Eliza said, her nose crinkling up. "He looks disgusting."

It was the face of pure evil and it made Jonah shiver. But at the same time he found himself unable to look away. Thankfully, Henry tapped him on the shoulder.

"Why don't you allow me to pull this stone aside? I think we may have found where they've taken your mother."

Jonah blinked hard a few times, snapping out of his long gaze at the image of Abaddon.

"Yeah, okay. Sure."

Henry leaned down and stuck his fingers in the holes around the edge of the stone and pulled. It didn't budge. He tried harder, straining with all of his angel-strength until Jonah thought his wings might pop off. It still didn't move.

He knelt over it, studying the stone more closely. As he ran his fingers softly over it, a look of concern grew on his face.

"We can't open this," he said. "It must be a Door of the Fallen. I've never seen one. But if this is what I think it is, it has been sealed with Abaddon's evil power. Only a fallen one can open it." He backed up and stood, arms folded, silently staring at the cover.

"Only a fallen one?" said Eliza. "But we have to get in. Our mom has to be somewhere behind this door. What are we supposed to do? Are we supposed to find some fallen angel hanging around who wants to help us destroy Abaddon's plan to bring the world down?" Jonah could tell she was getting to the end of her rope, waiting for an answer from Henry. He offered none.

They stood around the stone, staring at it silently.

Suddenly Jonah asked, curiously, "Are you sure that *only* a fallen one would be able to open this door?"

Henry cocked his head. "Yes, Jonah. It is known throughout the hidden realm that there are some doors that only those belonging to Abaddon, only the Fallen, can open."

Jonah, with a mysterious look in his eye, spoke softly. "What about someone who is . . . a *descendant* . . . of a fallen one?"

Henry began to nod slowly. "I see what you are saying. That just might work. But the one who tries needs to be very careful," he warned. "These things are never as simple as they might appear."

Jonah looked at Eliza. Before she could say anything, Jonah spoke up.

"Our grandfather is a fallen angel. I'll try."

He leaned down over the cover, took a deep breath, stuck his fingers into the holes, and began to pull.

"Aaaah!" he screamed. His hands suddenly felt like they were being held over an open flame. He snatched them away. He expected to see charred skin, or even bone, where his hands used to be. But his fingers looked totally fine.

"Jonah!" Eliza cried. "What is it?"

He continued looking at his fingers. "My hands. It felt like they were on fire."

Henry took his hands in his and looked at them. "They look, and feel, unharmed." He looked into Jonah's eyes, which had welled up with tears from the pain. "But there has to be another way to open this door!" muttered Henry. "There must be."

But there wasn't. And they all knew it.

"I'll try again," said Jonah.

Before Eliza or Henry could protest, Jonah reached down

again and stuck his fingers in the holes of the door. *Keep pulling. No matter what happens, just keep pulling.*

He closed his eyes again and pulled. His hands burned again—but there was more this time. Awful screams ripped through his ears, horrible sounds of people in pain. Wailing and cries of anguish filled his head, knifing down into his brain. Jonah's heart began to feel heavy, as rough and black as the stone cover he was pulling. His hands were still burning, and the screams caused despair to well up inside of him. His eyes popped open and he looked around, trying to see where the tortured voices were coming from. But there was no one except Eliza, watching him with concern, and Henry, bowing his head in fervent prayer.

Stand firm, Jonah.

It was just a whisper in his ear, though somehow louder than all of the wailing, which did not disappear, but seemed to have grown quieter.

Stand firm.

And then words came that pierced him down to his core: *Do not fear, Jonah. You are Mine.*

With these words the screams vanished, and his hands felt as if they had been thrust into a bucket of ice water. He sighed with relief, once again able to focus on trying to open the door. With a new energy coursing through his body, he pulled on the door with all his might. It began to move, rising slowly.

He heard Eliza's voice, urging him on. "You're doing it, Jonah! Keep pulling! The door is opening!"

His feet were grinding against the stone floor as the cover continued to move. It was heavier than anything he'd ever lifted, but finally he managed to pull it completely off and set it to the side. Collapsing on his knees, he wrapped his arms around his ribs and breathed deeply.

"Did you guys hear the . . . screams?" he asked, knowing what their answer would probably be.

Eliza knelt beside him and reached a motherly hand up to his forehead. "Are you feeling okay?"

"I'm fine," he said, pushing her hand away. He knew the look on his face said differently, though.

Only a fallen one could open this door.

Maybe he had heard Elohim's voice, but opening the door had proven something to Jonah, something that had been lurking in the back of his mind but that he'd been afraid to admit to himself: there was evil in him. There had been since the day he was born.

"There is no one beyond Elohim's reach," Henry said, reading Jonah's expression. Then he grinned. "Not even grandkids of the Fallen. Now I would suggest we see what's down here. What do you say?"

Henry went first, jumping down into the hole. Jonah was fine with that, since there was no sign of a floor below and he didn't have wings that could help him float down. He landed quickly, though, and Jonah could see his face only a few feet away.

"It's some sort of tunnel," Henry said. He made a throwing motion with his hands, and a white orb of light appeared in front of him.

Jonah could see the dirt floor now. He hopped down after Henry, then turned and helped Eliza drop down.

As his eyes adjusted to the light, he could see that they were in a small passageway that had been carved out of rock and dirt. Water dripped down the walls in various places, creating a dank smell and a mucky floor. It only led one direction.

"We're really going to go that way?" Eliza asked, looking down the dark tunnel as she tried to keep her voice from trembling.

Jonah didn't like it either, but he didn't see any other option. And he was certain that their mom—and the other nephilim—were somewhere at the end of this path.

As they made their way down the tunnel, Jonah's mind kept flashing back to the image on the door. Abaddon. Could they really rescue their mother from his grasp? If they could somehow get her, was there any way to escape, when fallen angels and monsters and who-knew-what-else were hiding in the dark corners of the hidden realm?

But then he remembered the voice he had heard not long ago. *Do not fear. Stand firm.* Was it really Elohim speaking into his ear? The words had brought him so much comfort. He thought about the last week of his life, how so much had changed, how he had discovered how special he really was, how he had seen the light of Elohim shining brightly from inside himself, and how Elohim's own angels had trusted him with this journey. The fear didn't matter right now. He was supposed to be here.

They plodded on silently along the small pathway, which seemed to go on forever. Jonah was starting to lose track of time. They could have been walking ten minutes, or it could have been hours. He didn't know anymore.

Henry suddenly grabbed Jonah's arm as they walked ahead into the darkness.

"Be prepared for anything." The worried look on his guardian angel's face didn't do anything to slow Jonah's racing heartbeat. "I have a feeling . . . just . . . be ready. They know we're here."

No sooner had he spoken those words than the floor began to

move underneath them, swirling as though it were liquid rather than hard stone.

"Aghh!" Eliza screamed, her knees sinking. "What's going on?"

Jonah watched as dirt-covered fingers began to reach up around her leg, emerging from the floor until an entire arm shot up and grabbed her tightly. Another one sprang up, latching firmly onto her other leg. She screamed again as the hands began pulling her down.

Instantly, more hands began to reach out of the ground toward them. Before Jonah could move, a hand wrapped around his ankle and pulled him to his knees. Another one grabbed his wrist, while yet another groped for his neck. It was the same with Henry. The hands had caught them all off guard, and they were sinking into the ground now, struggling to wriggle free.

Jonah tried to push the hands away, but they were too strong, and there were too many of them. Out of the corner of his eye he saw Henry fighting the hands, thrashing his body and wings around, and Eliza, whose entire leg had disappeared into the ground. This made him fight harder, but it seemed like the more he pulled, the worse it was. He felt the earth begin to open up underneath him and his leg slide into the sludge. His strength was useless, and with both arms pinned down now, he couldn't reach back to pull out an arrow. In a few seconds, it would be too late to do anything.

"Kids!"

Rolling his face to the side, Jonah saw Henry's head. It was the only part of him that was left above ground.

"Words," he cried out, as a hand grabbed the top of his head and tried to cover his mouth. "*The Word!*" He said it right before his head was yanked down into the muddy floor, disappearing from view.

Words? What did he mean? Jonah couldn't think clearly as he frantically wrestled with the slimy, unyielding hands.

"In the name of Elohim!" He heard Eliza's voice, weak at first, but then stronger. "For our battle is not against flesh and blood . . . in the name of Elohim, through His word, and by His power, I command you to release us!"

A shrieking sound came from somewhere under the ground, and immediately the hands released them. Eliza pulled a dirty leg from the clay, while Jonah leapt to his feet and tried to wipe the sticky mud off himself.

But Henry was nowhere to be seen.

"Henry!" Jonah shouted, dropping to his knees where Henry had sunk below the surface. Suddenly the dirt erupted, and Henry came spewing out like lava from a volcano, up into the air and back down again amid a rain of dirt clods. He stood up slowly, shaking the damp dirt from his body and wings, coughing clouds of dust into the air.

"Those were the Rephaim," Henry said between coughs. "Translated, it means the 'dead ones.' Like the Philistines you fought, they are bound to Abaddon, his commanders, and his minions, for all eternity. He controls them, and they do whatever he wishes. In fact, I'd be surprised if they weren't controlled by Marduk himself."

NINETEEN

VICTOR GRACE

W ho is that?" asked Eliza, resting against the tunnel wall.
"Abaddon has divided the world into eight regions,"
Henry answered. "Each region has a commander, responsible
for overseeing the battle there and creating as much mayhem as
possible, doing their part to keep people from turning to Elohim.
Marduk is the commander of this region, called the Second
Region, which encompasses most of North America. The Second
Region is a key area in the angelic rebellion. Marduk is a very
powerful and extremely dangerous fallen one. No doubt he is the
one behind the kidnapping of your mother."

The tunnel was gradually getting larger, and a dim, bluish
glow came from an opening ahead. Henry quickly extinguished
his light. He motioned them silently forward, and they moved out
of the mouth of the tunnel into what looked like another basement.

In front of them was a stack of old wooden crates, and they
crouched behind them quietly. Faded words were stamped on
each one.

New York City Asylum for the Insane
Wards Island, New York

Eliza read the words slowly. "We're in a . . . mental hospital, or something?"

"Ahh," Henry said, like he was remembering something. "I've heard of this place."

Jonah leaned in. "Where are we exactly?"

"These boxes are old," he said in a low voice. "This used to be the New York City Asylum for the Insane, or rather, somewhere underneath it. Now it's called the Manhattan Psychiatric Center. We must have crossed under the river and are now on Wards Island, under the old hospital that houses mentally ill patients. It's also popped up recently as being a hot spot."

Jonah looked at him blankly.

"A lot of potential fallen angel activity going on," he explained. "Not long ago—a hundred years or so—this was a hotbed for Abaddon's activity in the Second Region. A headquarters, if you will. It was a stronghold of his, which made sense—there were so many Fallen here, tormenting so many people. It has been quiet for the past several decades, but recently there's been a spike in reported activity."

He talked about years like they were days, and Jonah had to remember that to an eternal being, that's probably what it felt like.

"But I don't remember hearing about a lower level to this place," Henry continued. "It must have been well hidden."

Jonah stepped forward and looked through a crevice between a couple of the boxes. He breathed out hard through his teeth as he peered through the crack. It was exactly what he had seen in his vision. A large, dirty room lit by fluorescent lights that reminded him of the old Peacefield Memorial Hospital where he'd visited church members with his dad. He'd always felt awful for the poor people who had to stay in such a depressing place, but this was somehow even worse. A few of the lights flickered on and off, buzzing and sputtering their garish light around the room. The walls were grimy tiles that probably used to be white, but were now covered with patches of greenish mold. The floor was cracked cement, with a drain in the center.

Eight old hospital beds lined the sides of the room. A person was tied to each bed by old leather straps; only one bed was empty. Cupped over the top of each person was an electric shield.

The nephilim.

Abaddon's plan was almost complete. He just needed the last one.

And then Jonah spotted his mother.

He had to blink hard to hold back tears and bite his tongue to keep from crying out to her. She looked unconscious, or close to it, like the rest of the people around her. Jonah remembered looking into her eyes in his vision and tried to focus on the fact that she was still alive. He only wished that the vision he'd seen had been real, that somehow his mom would know that he was coming for her and he would save her, no matter what.

Guards were standing with spears in front of each nephilim, while the rest of the Fallen were swarming around the room like worker bees.

"Do you see her?" Jonah asked Eliza, moving to let her look through the crack. Eliza gave a quick nod, but looked like she might explode if she opened her mouth.

"They look like they're waiting," Henry said, watching the movements of the Fallen from behind the crates.

"For one more nephilim to arrive," answered Jonah.

At that moment, a rusty metal door was shoved open on the other side of the room. They jumped at the crash of the door against the tile wall.

"I don't think they are going to have to wait any longer," said Eliza. "Look."

They watched as four fallen ones entered the room one after the other, brandishing spears and swords. Behind them, a dark-skinned woman in a purple dress with short-cropped blond hair was being dragged by her arms across the cement. Like the others, her body was limp and her head was drooping. Two fallen ones were pulling her, and another one grunted and pointed toward the eighth holding bed. They took her there and yanked her up by her arms with such force that her head snapped back and she cried out in pain, saying something in a language that sounded African. Quickly they secured the leather straps around her wrists. One of the Fallen came forward and pointed two fingers toward her. Electricity came out of his fingertips, surrounding the woman and creating a shield around her.

"They've got her. The eighth nephilim," Jonah said. He glanced over at Eliza, who was staring at the gathering in horror. Henry had grown steely-eyed, a determined look on his face.

Eliza's voice quivered in the darkness. "What are they going to do to them?"

Jonah clenched his fists, and when he spoke, there was decisiveness in his voice. "We're not going to wait around to find out."

He turned to the guardian angel. "You ready for this, Henry?"

Henry, his gaze still locked on the fallen angels, answered, "I'm ready."

But then he turned to Jonah and Eliza, looking at them with concern. "But that room . . . it's no place for kids. It might be best if you two stay here and let me go on without you now." Jonah could see Henry's guardian-angel nature kicking in before his eyes.

"Are you kidding?" said Eliza, wiping an angry tear from her cheek. "And I suppose you have a plan that doesn't include us?"

Henry didn't answer.

"You need us," she said. "Look how many of them there are! And look at what we just made it through. Together."

Henry held up two hands in protest. "No one is saying you haven't done a great deal. You have."

"Glad to hear you say that, my guardian angel friend," Jonah said, placing a hand on Henry's shoulder. "Because I actually *do* have a plan."

They huddled together behind the stacks of boxes, and Jonah shared his plan with them. Henry stroked his chin thoughtfully.

"You know," he said, "this just might work."

"It's going to be our only shot," Eliza said, looking up at him. "So it had better."

"Ready, Henry?" Jonah asked.

The angel nodded, then moved past the boxes, standing tall, wings outstretched. He wasn't hiding anymore. He wanted to be seen, so he stood and waited.

He didn't have to wait for long.

A fallen one suddenly screeched, a noise like a hundred fingernails grating against a blackboard, causing Jonah and Eliza to slap their hands over their ears. The creature waved his finger at Henry, and the other fallen angels turned, dozens of pairs of yellow eyes trained in their direction.

Henry's wings stiffened and he stormed forward, stringing his bow.

A red flaming arrow soared past Henry, and Jonah and Eliza ducked behind the boxes again. Jonah heard a roar as flashes of light began to bounce off the ceiling. The fight was on.

"That's our signal," Jonah said. "Time to go!"

Jonah and Eliza scooted around the boxes, away from the blasts that were erupting in the room. Henry was playing his part, drawing the attention—and fire—of the Fallen. They dove behind a cement column and surveyed the situation again.

"I think it's working!" said Eliza. "They're chasing him!"

The fallen angels who had been milling around were suddenly focused on the intruder. Henry's arrows were flying quickly, fallen ones hitting the ground and then disintegrating. The Fallen were raining their own flaming arrows down on him, but so far he had been able to avoid getting hit. All of the fallen ones were moving quickly in the direction of the angel, and even the ones who were guarding the nephilim left their posts and joined the others.

Some of them had spread their wings and were off the ground, fighting from midair. Henry began to back up, just as they had discussed. The fallen ones pursued him. He was getting pushed back—or rather, letting himself get pushed back—into the tunnel entrance.

Finally, Henry retreated into the tunnel, the Fallen following him there.

Jonah and Eliza watched as every last guard disappeared

through the doorway, hungry for the battle, eager to spill angel blood. No one noticed them enter the room.

They ran by two nephilim, strapped to beds and caged with the energy shields. On the left was a tall, redheaded man in a mud-covered business suit, sprawled limply on the bed. To the right was an Asian woman in a simple brown dress, just as dirty, lying the same way behind the glowing shield.

Eliza paused in front of the woman, but Jonah pulled her arm as he hurried past.

"Come on, Eliza!" he whispered urgently.

"But . . . these people—"

"There's no time!" Jonah barked, dragging her with him. "We have to get Mom!"

Eliza shook her head and jerked her arm from his, but said, "Okay!" and hurried behind him until they were in front of their mother.

"Remember," Jonah said, "don't touch the shield—or force field, whatever this is . . ." His voice fell as he saw his mother close up. Her head still lay across her shoulder, her eyes closed, but puffy and bruised. The cut that he had seen in his vision looked deeper now than it had appeared, more jagged across her cheek.

"Mom!" Eliza whispered desperately through the translucent shield. "Can you hear me, Mom? It's Eliza! Are you there?"

She did not move. Jonah's mind flashed with visions of his mom from the past. Images of her walking him to school on his first day of kindergarten, of standing in the kitchen flipping pancakes, reading him a book at night—all the memories came flooding in. As he looked at his mother now, beaten, trapped, silent—he started to feel very sick to his stomach. Was she unconscious, passed out from the abuse she had taken, or the lack of water and food? Maybe she was just asleep. Or maybe . . . he stopped, unwilling to let his mind think that maybe it was too late.

"Mom!" he cried. He knew he was being loud, but right now he didn't care. "Mom!"

"Jonah! Keep it down!" Eliza scolded in a hoarse whisper.

Jonah kept shouting. "Mom! You have to wake up! We came to get you, and you have to come home now." Tears began to roll down his cheeks. "We need you, Mom! You can't leave us. You can't go away. We need you. I need you. I love you, Mom."

Slowly, Eleanor raised her head and fluttered her eyelids weakly. She stared with her eyes half-open, trying to focus. Looking hazily at them, she finally realized who was in front of her.

"J-Jonah?" she said weakly. "Eliza? What are you . . . ?"

She was alive!

Eleanor opened her mouth and tried to say something else, but no words would come out.

"Don't try to talk," said Jonah. "Just wait until we get out of here. There'll be plenty of time to talk then."

He felt a new surge of energy. His mother was alive! But she was not going anywhere unless they could get her out from behind that shield. Henry had given them specific instructions on how to release her. He just prayed that it worked.

"It's your turn now, E," Jonah said.

Eliza looked nervous, but took two steps back and raised her hands slowly above her head. Immediately, she generated a shield of her own, of bright white light, extending from her fingertips to the ground. She began to move forward, until her shield and the one guarding her mother were almost touching. She glanced at Jonah, who nodded to her. Closing her eyes, she took one big step forward.

The shields collided, and a giant buzzing sound filled their ears. It reminded Jonah of the mosquito zapper they had on their back porch at home, except it was about a thousand times louder. Sparks flew, and Eliza was thrown onto her back. But both shields had disappeared, cancelling each other out.

Eliza lay on the ground for a few seconds, staring straight up at the fluorescent lights, dazed. But she quickly pushed herself up on her elbows, straightening her glasses.

Jonah and Eliza embraced their mom quickly, and then Jonah spun around to see if they had been heard. Blasts of light and flame shot from the tunnel. The intense battle was still raging between Henry and the Fallen. Somehow he was still holding them off, distracting them so that even the explosion created by the shields colliding hadn't drawn any attention.

They had to move fast, and they still had the straps on their mom's arms and legs to undo.

"Oh, Jonah," his mother said, smiling weakly as he turned to face her again.

He grinned back. "Hold still for one second, would you?"

Her eyes grew big as he pulled the arrow seemingly from nowhere behind his back, and the bow appeared in his left hand. The white arrow glistened in the dark room as he held the point close to her wrist. Before she could protest or pull away, he swiped the tip of the arrow across the leather straps. They fell to the ground immediately. Moving over to her other arm, he did the same thing, and then he cut the bindings on her feet as well. When they pulled Eleanor up off the bed, she fell against Jonah, who caught her in his arms and propped her up.

"My dear children," she said, "my dear children . . . you came . . ." She placed her hand on Eliza's cheek and rubbed it softly.

"Of course we did," said Jonah, continuing to look back over his shoulder every few seconds. "And now, we need to get you out of here."

She held up a finger as she leaned against him. "The others," she said, as she coughed loudly. "We can't leave the others."

She motioned toward the remaining seven nephilim, trapped behind their shields. They all still lay unconscious, just as she had been. The battle continued to blaze in the tunnel, but Jonah knew Henry wouldn't be able to hold them for much longer. Soon, one of the Fallen would figure out that this was nothing more than a distraction and turn around.

"Mom," he protested, "we don't have time to rescue all of these people. We have to get you out of here . . . *now*."

"Jonah," she said quietly but firmly, "they have children too. Just like you. We can't just leave them here for the Fallen and Abaddon. They'll never see the light of day again. And his plan . . ." She broke off in another fit of coughing before she could finish. Even though her voice was still weak, Jonah heard the determination behind her words and knew she would never leave willingly until they had freed every last nephilim.

He looked at Eliza. "Come on, E. Let's do this. And fast."

Her arms were already raised, and Jonah followed her as she produced the shield and ran it into the ones covering the captured nephilim. Each time it knocked her back, but she was learning to steady herself and keep her feet. Jonah kept his bow and arrow ready, so that each time she destroyed the protective shield, he was immediately there to break through the straps.

They freed the African woman with the blond hair, the Asian woman, and then the man in the business suit. All three stumbled as they got up, falling against the wall behind them, but they soon steadied themselves and were able to walk, with some help from Eleanor.

Jonah and Eliza were approaching the next bed, which was holding a tall man wearing a Russian fur hat, when a fiery arrow slammed into the wall above them, raining shards of rock and dust on top of them. Turning quickly, they saw a fallen one standing in the entrance to the tunnel, restringing his bow to shoot again. His grotesque, scaly face smiled wickedly, his giant muscles rippling as he pulled the arrow back and took aim at Jonah's head.

He let it fly, but Eliza was quicker. Her shield deflected the arrow, and it landed harmlessly on the ground, quickly turning into a tiny pile of black dust.

"Thanks!" Jonah shouted, but his eyes were drawn beyond the first fallen one, to the growing number of others behind him. The big one was screeching at all the rest, and Jonah knew what he must be saying. *It's a trap! The nephilim are escaping. Come back!*

"They're headed our way!" Jonah cried out to Eliza and his mom. *"Run!"*

But there was nowhere to run. They were against a wall, and a fallen angel had quickly blocked their access to the metal door. The only other way out was the tunnel, and that was out of the question. The only thing they could do now was pull behind the safety of Eliza's shield, squeezing tightly together as they tried to fit both themselves and the three other freed nephilim inside the protective bubble. At least half of the Fallen had poured back out of the tunnel, the others continuing to fight the severely outnumbered Henry.

All of them concentrated their arrows on Eliza's shield, and she began to take a barrage of hits. Her arms remained in the air, but she was struggling, and each blow pushed her back just a little more. Soon they were almost against the wall, and the arrows continued to pelt them from every direction.

"Eliza!" Jonah said, as she knelt on one knee, still holding her arms up, but just barely. His mom was beside her with her head bowed, praying, but she looked weaker by the second, and he knew she could not make it much longer in her current state. The shield began to flicker, and Jonah began to wonder what it would feel like to get hit by a flaming arrow. He looked at his mom and sister kneeling there on the hard cement, and realized how much he loved both of them, and how he wished he could tell them that now. But it was too late.

In just a few seconds, they were all going to die.

Jonah looked past the fallen ones, trying to spot Henry. A line of the Fallen were coming closer, but there was no sign of him anywhere. Whatever was happening in the tunnel, their guardian angel would be of no help now.

Just as Eliza's shield disappeared, a large fallen angel, taller and even more muscular than the rest, stepped forward and briefly held his hand up. All of the arrows immediately stopped. His yellow eyes glared at them, and he smiled arrogantly, showing them his jagged, black teeth. His hands were on his hips, and steam blew from his nostrils. His skin was crusty and covered in scales, and when he stretched his crumply wings out to their full span, even some of the Fallen retreated a step back in fear.

He pointed to the three dazed nephilim who were crouching behind Eleanor, grunted some orders, and immediately three heavily armored fallen ones came and snatched them away, slapping glowing wrist and feet cuffs on them. He walked forward and then passed by each of them, glaring down at Jonah and Eliza, before standing in front of Eleanor.

"Eleanor Stone," he sneered, "stand up." She remained on the floor. "I said, stand up!" She slowly rose to her feet in front of the giant fallen one.

"Do you know who I am?" he said.

She shook her head. "I don't know your name," she said, meeting his eyes with her own defiant stare, "but I do know that you are a *fallen* angel."

He threw his head back and laughed. "Oh, but I am so . . . much . . . *more*." He roared so loudly that it shook rocks loose from the tunnel opening and they tumbled down into the room across the concrete floor. "I am Marduk. Commander of the Second Region of Abaddon."

Eleanor simply glared at him and folded her arms, clearly unimpressed.

"But perhaps," he said, suddenly morphing into a tall, handsome gentleman with dark hair and a goatee, wearing a brown suit and a matching hat, "this is who you'd rather meet." He extended his hand and smiled warmly.

Eleanor grew as pale as moonlight. The man standing before her was the same smiling man posing with her mother in the old, faded picture. The picture of her father.

"I am Victor Grace," he said, beaming at Eleanor. "It's a pleasure to finally meet you, my oh-so-special *daughter*."

TWENTY

Family Reunion

J onah looked at Marduk—or Victor Grace?—then back at his mother. This fallen angel was Jonah and Eliza's grandfather. Ever since his parents had told him how his mother was born a nephilim, he had known that his grandfather was a fallen one. But to come this close to him, to feel the evil dripping out of the pores of his skin, made Jonah's stomach queasy. His mother and his grandfather stared each other down, and he saw his mom straighten her back again and regain her footing.

"I wondered if we would ever meet, *Marduk*," Eleanor said, and even in this filthy place, covered with dirt and blood, Jonah saw her quiet confidence start to rise back to the surface. Her arms were crossed, and he remembered where Eliza got her stubbornness from.

Marduk brushed a speck of dirt off of his shoulder and slid a hand into his suit pocket. "Oh, Eleanor, I knew this day was coming. After all, why else would we have taken such care to put our little plan in place? Why else would we waste time wooing you pathetic, weak-willed humans? Winning your mother over was so demeaning, to have to stoop to her level, to pretend like I loved her. She was so needy, so empty, so void of purpose in her life. And I had what she thought she so desperately needed. I filled that hole in her measly heart." His grin distorted his face, which was full of hateful pride and rage. Stroking the beard on his chin, he continued on.

"Everything was in preparation for this day, the day we would finally be reunited, Eleanor, don't you see? Of course you do. You know that now. But you didn't see it coming, did you? We were patient. Our plan was too clever for even *His* pesky warrior-angels to detect." Even though he had taken on the look of a stately gentleman, his voice seethed, full of the evil of a fallen angel.

"But you will all find out today why you are here," he said, turning to look at all of the captives. "We have big plans for each of you. World-altering plans, dreamed up in the mind of Abaddon himself. And each one of you is going to play your part perfectly."

"That will never happen, Marduk!" Jonah suddenly shouted. "My mom will never give in to you and your evil plans! You don't know her."

Marduk pursed his lips and put his hand to his chin, tapping one finger on his mouth, as if in deep thought. "You know, *grandson*, I am actually glad you and your sister are here today too. I'm thrilled that you have come and made your ridiculous little attempt to free your mother and all the rest of them. Because I want you to see what is going to happen, to witness history. I want you to see your mother turn to Abaddon, pledge her allegiance to him, and promise forever to do his bidding." He toyed with his goatee playfully. "It's what their breed does, after all, being half-fallen. So powerful, yet so easily swayed toward their darker desires. It will be good for the two of you to see how *useful* your mother can be. Before you die, that is."

Jonah was furious, about to respond, when his mother did something that caught his attention. She slipped her hands behind her back as Marduk was talking, continuing to stare at him but fumbling with something in her fingers.

In her right hand, a glowing ball the size of a baseball appeared, an orb of green light that looked like it was spinning in her palm. Marduk had turned away to give his fallen ones a cocky glance, and that was all the time she needed.

She flung the ball of light at Marduk, and it sailed through the air like a major-league fastball, catching him squarely on the back. As it hit him, it exploded, blasting him into the crowd of the Fallen gathered around. He was sprawled out facedown on the hard floor, unmoving. The creatures around him wailed, and more than a dozen of them raised flaming arrows and spears, preparing to fire them at her.

"Wait."

Marduk moved slowly, raising his hand from the floor, and reluctantly they dropped their weapons. Smoke was rising from his back as he picked himself up off of the floor, still in the image of Victor. "We can't kill the nephilim, no matter how satisfying it would be. Boss's orders.

"Besides," he continued as he slapped the dirt off of his jacket and straightened his tie, "after Abaddon gets through with her, she could be the world's next great dictator. And we wouldn't want to spoil that, would we?"

"We can, however, have a little fun," he growled. "After all, we never did have a chance to play catch, did we, daughter? You know, spend a little family time together? Maybe that's why your aim is so bad." He laughed scornfully. "Let's see if you can catch any better than you can throw, shall we?"

Marduk charged at Eleanor, his yellow eyes breaking through the calm blue ones he wore as Victor. He ran headlong into her, with the intention of slamming her into the wall. But she quickly dug her heel down into a large crack in the cement floor and, in one deft move, caught hold of his head, spun around, and used his momentum against him, throwing him into the wall instead.

"All right, Mom!" Eliza said, tapping Jonah on the arm excitedly. "Did you see that?"

"Oh yeah," he said, smiling at his mother in awe. "I think Marduk picked on the wrong nephilim today."

Marduk growled fiercely at Eleanor, who had outmatched him twice now, in front of all the Fallen under his command. Jonah thought he could almost see Marduk's skin boiling with rage, but then he watched in dismay as his body suddenly became fluid, a dark cloud of particles. The cloud zoomed through the air so fast Jonah could barely see it, and in one breath, it was behind Eleanor. Before she realized what was happening, Marduk had turned solid again and crashed his fist down across her neck.

Jonah watched his mother crumple to the ground. He tried to run toward her, but one of the creatures jumped out in front of him, sticking a flaming arrow in his face, daring him to take another step toward his mother. A dozen others had drawn their bows and held their arrows aimed toward Jonah and Eliza, itching for an excuse to let them fly.

Eleanor shook her head a few times as she faced the floor, dazed. Marduk stood over her, gloating. He shifted back into Victor Grace, reached down and grabbed her by the hair, and spoke in a soft, gentle voice. "You are a powerful nephilim, there's no doubt about that. But let's just remember who your daddy is, shall we?" He slung her head toward the floor and stood up, morphing into his fallen angel form again. "Tie her back up."

Two nasty-looking fallen angels grabbed her and slammed her back against the wall, securing her hands and feet with their electrical chains.

There was a new determination in Marduk's eyes now. He turned to one of the nephilim, the one dressed in the suit, and beckoned him over. The fallen ones freed him from his restraints and, walking reluctantly to the middle of the room, he stood inches away from the commander. Jonah had never seen a grown man shake and twitch so much before.

"Your name?" growled Marduk. The man stammered, staring down at his shoes, anywhere but at him.

"I...uh...I..."

"You have forgotten your name, nephilim?" he jeered.

The man finally looked up. "R-Roger, sir, Marduk, sir," he said feebly. "Roger C-C-Clamwater."

Marduk smiled reassuringly. "Roger Clamwater, look at me." Roger continued to look down. "Look at me!" As he said this, he raised his finger, and Roger's head snapped up, like a puppet. "That's right, Mr. Clamwater," he said soothingly. "Look into my eyes. Just like that."

Jonah watched as the man locked eyes with Marduk for several seconds. The color began to drain out of the man's face. The fallen angel grabbed the nephilim on each side of his head and held it even closer to his own, staring him down with his terrifying yellow eyes. Jonah looked on in horrified silence. Marduk's lips were moving, just slightly, as he continued. Finally, he released the man and the gaze was broken. The nephilim dropped to one knee and lowered his head.

"My lord."

When the man looked up, his eyes were black, like shadows. The trembling was gone, replaced by a confident smirk now stamped across his face. A few of the nephilim gasped. The man walked over toward the fallen ones and stood in front of them, hands behind his back, awaiting his new master's next command.

"See now," Marduk said comfortably, "that wasn't so difficult, was it?"

Another nephilim was released and pushed forward— this time it was the large Russian. He looked terrified, but was unable to resist. Marduk repeated what he had done with the first nephilim, staring down into his eyes, mouthing some unknown words, and then the Russian bowed, pledging his allegiance to the Evil One.

What is he saying to them? Jonah thought. *What could make these innocent people change from being scared out of their wits to being so . . . evil?*

Jonah watched in disbelief as the same thing happened one by one with each of the next five nephilim. All were dragged before Marduk unwillingly, looking ready to die from fright, but afterward, they just as readily gave themselves over to him. Seven of them stood behind Marduk now, neat as robots in a row, hanging on his every word, waiting for him to tell them what to do next.

There was only one left.

"Eleanor?" he cooed softly, extending his grotesque hand toward her. As he did, he transformed into Victor Grace again— her father, reaching his hand out to his daughter.

She paused for a few seconds, but very slowly began to walk to the middle of the room. Jonah grabbed her arm.

"No, Mom!" he screamed. "No! You can't do this!" She looked at him briefly, her eyes full of fear and sadness, but somehow vacant too. She didn't say anything as she pried his fingers from around her arm. Eliza was still leaning against the wall in a daze, watching. "No!"

But she kept walking, until she was standing face-to-face with Marduk again, who wore a sickening smile as he looked down at her like a hawk at a mouse.

"I knew you would come around, Eleanor."

Just as those words left his lips, an arrow came hurtling toward his skull. Without looking, he reached up in a blur and grabbed the white arrow in the palm of his hand, snatching it out of the air. With one hand he snapped it in two and threw it down on the floor.

Jonah stood holding his bow, breathing sharply, his heart about to race out of his chest.

"I have had enough of you, boy!" he said, turning away from Eleanor and stomping toward Jonah. Before he could pull out another arrow and fire it, Marduk was in front of him, and Jonah felt his strong fingers clamp around his arm like a vise.

Turning to look up, Jonah's eyes met those of the fallen angel, and the room around them began to disappear.

TWENTY-ONE

NEW YORK CITY ASYLUM
FOR THE INSANE

The room, like a wall of blocks kicked over all at once, had fallen away. Jonah's mom and sister were gone. The other nephilim and the Fallen were nowhere to be seen. Jonah found himself lying facedown on a white-tiled floor, which smelled like a combination of industrial cleaner and his middle school gym. Picking himself up, he realized he was standing in a long hallway. The walls and ceiling were also white, lit by those same fluorescent lights.

An old man stumbled toward him, holding himself up on a rolling walker. He stared vacantly at something behind Jonah, his mouth hanging slightly open. Jonah glanced over his shoulder, but there was nothing there. Ahead of him, a thin woman walked down the hallway, her shoulders hunched over. On her back, a fallen angel was perched, its claws digging into the back of her head.

It didn't click with him that he must be upstairs, in the asylum,

217

until an overweight doctor in a white lab coat turned the corner, stared at him, and wrote something on a clipboard as he walked straight through him. Jonah felt the electric jolt of his soul briefly connecting with the doctor's.

He began to move down the hallway, which was lined with rooms, keypad locks on the outside of each metal door. Somehow Marduk had transported him here, and he had to figure out how to get back downstairs.

Just as he spotted the stairwell, a man in a brown suit, hat, and goatee came around the corner, smirking at him. Victor Grace.

He stood with his arms folded for one long minute, sizing up the thirteen-year-old boy who had the guts to try to shoot him with a flaming arrow. Then he lifted off his hat and ran his fingers through his hair, pushing it back neatly.

Jonah tried to muster up his courage, but he stuttered a little when he spoke. "W-w-what have you done with everybody? W-where is my family?"

"They are all downstairs, waiting for us to return—safe and sound, Jonah, safe and sound. I just thought, Jonah, that you and I could use a little . . . one-on-one time together. Since we're not quite seeing *eye to eye*." He chuckled as he took a few steps toward him. "Abaddon's going to be here soon, you see, boy. And I can't have you getting in the way of our plans any longer."

The sound of someone beating on the locked door beside him made Jonah jump. Through the small glass windowpane he saw a desperate face staring right at him, shouting something, hammering on the door with his fists. Just over his shoulder, he could make out the twisted, darkened face of a fallen angel, grinning wickedly.

Victor wore the same evil smile on his face. "We've made lots of friends in this place over the years. Lots of vulnerable minds to twist and turn, to reshape into our own image."

Jonah shivered, feeling a chill in his soul from standing so close to Marduk. It was more intense than any blizzard he could imagine.

"What do you want from me? Why are we here?" Jonah fired the questions at him, both nerves and anger exploding in his voice.

"That is *the* question, Jonah, isn't it?" said Marduk. "What do *we* want?" He took a step toward Jonah. "A very simple answer to that, of course. What we want, Jonah, is *Jonah*. We want you."

Even though Jonah tried his best to appear confident, he was shaking, his stomach tying itself into knots. The chief commander of the Second Region—of most of the *continent*—Marduk himself, who also happened to be his grandfather, had his eyes trained on him, and all he could think about was that he was just a kid from Peacefield, New Jersey. What was he doing here? Everything had happened so fast.

"You are afraid, *grandson*," the fallen angel said, sneering. "You should be. You are alone. Your mother isn't here to protect you, nor your father, nor your sister. It's just you. And when this is all over, just like all the other nephilim, *you and your mother are going to bow to Abaddon*."

Jonah wished there was something he could do. But he had already proven that arrows were useless. The strength that he had as a quarterling would be pathetic compared to Marduk's, and if he tried to fight, he would probably end up dead. His mind spun frantically. He looked around the hallway, for any kind of answer. What could he possibly do with this powerful fallen one focusing all of his power on him?

I am with you, Jonah.

He blinked, and his mind suddenly quieted. It was the voice, the same one he had heard before. He thought he had been hearing Elohim's voice speaking to him before, but he wasn't positive.

Now, deep inside his soul, he was certain.

Trust Me, came the voice again, a clear beacon amid the chaos of Jonah's thoughts; it sounded as loud as if someone were standing beside him, speaking into his ear.

I am not alone. Jonah pressed this truth into his heart.

Marduk wanted him to feel like he was alone, like no one was there for him, like everyone had either turned on him or was helpless. But there was Someone who was there beside him. He would always be there, whether at school, on a subway, or in a mental hospital, facing one of the fiercest fallen angels on the planet.

Elohim was there, He always would be there, and He was reminding Jonah of that right now.

I hear You, Elohim, Jonah said inside his heart. *I do trust You. With everything I have, I trust You. And I need You right now, more than ever.*

His hands suddenly steadied, his stomach stopped lurching, and his mind became peaceful and focused. Marduk glared at him, but Jonah breathed in slowly. He exhaled. He did it again, breathing deep and letting it out. Somehow he knew that though he was in the presence of Abaddon's underlord, he was even deeper in the presence of Elohim Himself, the God who created everything and the One who had everything under His control.

His fear left him. It vanished. Jonah shoved his hands in his pockets, met Victor Grace's stare with his own, and waited. He even felt a slight smile crease the corners of his mouth. Elohim would show him what to do next.

Victor held his arms away from his body and transformed

into who he really was again: the dark fallen angel. The back of the angel's hand came so fast Jonah didn't see it. Cracking his fingers across Jonah's jaw, it sent him crashing to the ground.

"Wipe that grin off your face, boy!" he roared, and moved in again. The force of Marduk's next blow sent Jonah all the way across the tile floor, his head slamming against the wall. He looked up and blinked a few times. The lights above him were spinning, coming in and out of focus. He felt a warm rush of liquid oozing down the side of his face. Somewhere far away, he heard the sound of Marduk's laughter rise over the pounding in his head.

Jonah shook his head and forced himself up off the ground, kneeling now on one knee, grabbing at a doorknob to steady himself.

"Well, well, well," Marduk said. "I am glad you are coming to your senses, young Jonah. I told you that in the end you would have no choice but to bow." He took two steps forward, his face twisted with pulsing hatred, and extended a hand to Jonah.

In that moment Jonah did the only thing he could think of to do. He ran forward, summoning all of the strength he had, and plowed himself into the fallen one. Skillfully, Marduk moved to the side and jammed a fist into his stomach. He felt himself hurtle into the air and turn upside down.

"Don't waste your energy fighting me, my dear boy," Marduk said. "You're just putting off the inevitable. I brought your mother into this world, knowing the day would come when she, and all the others like her, would begin to do our bidding." He chuckled, and then added, "So if you think about it, Jonah, I brought you into the world too."

Jonah slowly stood up and managed to calmly smile while he secretly scanned the hallway for a way out. He had to get away, get back to his mother and his sister and Henry. As he slowly back-stepped away from Marduk, he caught a flash of red out of the corner of his eye: an exit sign above the stairwell door.

"It may be true that you are my grandfather, and there's nothing I can do about that," he said, taking a few steps backward as he talked. "But your plan has backfired, Marduk. Want to know why? Everyone in my family loves Elohim. And you know what? *I belong to Him.*"

With that, Jonah bolted through the door, summoning all his physical strength as his basketball shoes turned into his speedy sandals in the nick of time.

The stairs were in front of him, and he had a decision to make. Up or down.

The draw of going down the steps was strong. It would bring him back to his family. But bring Marduk with him.

The only thing certain about going upstairs was that he would be on his own.

In an instant, he had made his choice. As fast as he could, he began to climb. He passed two patients, who were, of course, completely unaware of his presence. Round and round the stairwell he went, counting at least ten levels, until he reached a small door that said RESTRICTED: MANHATTAN PSYCHIATRIC CENTER ROOF ACCESS.

He pushed through it and found himself standing on top of the building. But before he could get his bearings, a hand grabbed him by the back of the neck and threw him across the top of the roof. He thudded into the low wall that surrounded the edge of the building, the wind knocked out of him.

"Really, Jonah?" Marduk said, walking toward him. "Did you really think you could outrun me?"

Jonah gasped, trying desperately to catch his breath and push himself up so that he could at least draw an arrow. Or do something. *Anything.*

But Marduk was too quick. He had him by both shoulders, his face inches away from Jonah's.

"Enough games!" the fallen angel said. But then, with cool charm in his voice, "This is officially your last chance. Bend your knee to Abaddon, and you can have everything your little heart desires. And I mean *everything*. You can be rich beyond anything you've imagined. And think about this: you could be the king of your school, the captain of your basketball team, whatever you want. Everyone will like you. And that's just for starters."

Cocking his evil face sideways, he studied with piercing eyes the young man pressed back against the concrete wall.

"Or," he said, emotionless, "you can die. Live and make history. Or die without anyone knowing. What's it going to be?"

The pull of Marduk's eyes was intense. The words came once again, though, from inside Jonah, but loudly in his ears:

Do you trust Me?

He closed his eyes. The words of Elohim.

Jonah looked up again and met Marduk's yellow eyes. He smiled.

"I already told you," said Jonah. "I belong to Elohim."

Marduk screamed, and he flung the boy as hard as he could.

Jonah tumbled over the rooftop wall, and down.

TWENTY-TWO

Blade of Angels

Jonah fell through the air feeling as though he were falling in slow motion. He had experienced a lot of dreams where he was falling, and each time he was screaming at the top of his lungs. As he fell for real, though, he did not think to scream at all. It was a remarkably quiet couple of seconds. Like a rock thrown off a bridge, he fell silently, growing closer to the ground with each passing second. He wondered what it would feel like to die. He would not have to wait long to find out.

And then, out of the corner of his eye, Jonah saw a flash of white light streaking toward him. He was preparing himself for the landing, crashing down onto the pavement below, being smashed to bits. Instead, something grabbed his shoulders, clamping around them tightly. His feet scraped the concrete, but not the rest of him. Suddenly, he noticed he was flying over a group of trees. Two strong hands held his shoulders. He looked above him, saw the silver wings shining, and realized that he was being carried along through the air by an angel.

Am I dreaming? The angel looked down at him but said nothing, and as Jonah gazed ahead, he realized for the first time how fast they were moving. The angel's wings flapped a few times, propelling them faster and higher, riding the wind until they were well above the city, and the building he had been thrown from was only a speck behind them.

I'm not going to die after all, he thought.

"Whoo-hoo!" he screamed, raising a fist into the air. His chest filled up with a mixture of excitement, joy, and relief, so much that he thought his heart was going to explode.

They had left land behind and were now over water. In the distance, he spotted what looked like an outcropping of land that they were heading toward.

A cliff rose before them, and on top of the cliff was a giant tree, rounded by lush, green leaves and huge branches. Behind the tree, as far as Jonah could see, were miles and miles of fields covered with wildflowers. They landed softly on a grassy spot just beyond the cliff's edge.

The angel stood majestically in front of Jonah, and he could not help but feel in awe. He was just as tall as the angel Marcus, and was covered with sleek, metallic armor. His wings looked razor-blade sharp. A glittering sword hung from his belt.

"Do you know who I am, Jonah?" the angel asked.

Jonah struggled to find any words to say. Finally, it dawned on him. "Archangel Michael?"

The warrior angel nodded. Behind his stony, serious expression, Jonah saw kind, twinkling eyes.

"Your trust in Elohim is to be commended," Michael said. "He asked me to bring you here."

Jonah's brow wrinkled. Michael didn't say anything else but glanced at the tree, ushering him toward it.

He wondered again how this was possible, but if it was some kind of dream, he had not woken up yet. Jonah began to walk toward the massive tree. He looked back over his shoulder and saw Michael standing still, a statue on the side of the cliff, watching him intently.

Jonah figured that if the rest of his family were there, they could not together reach all the way around the trunk. Beautifully gnarled roots ran off in all directions from the base. He approached it tentatively, glanced back over his shoulder again, and received a reassuring nod from the angel.

He began to walk around the trunk to the other side when something glittered, grabbing his attention. A large, silver sword was sticking between the roots, beside the trunk. It reminded him of the one he had seen Michael wearing on his belt. It had a carved golden handle and a long, silver blade. As he looked closer, he saw words imprinted along the blade, and he stooped down to read them.

FOR THE WORD OF GOD IS ALIVE AND ACTIVE. SHARPER THAN ANY DOUBLE-EDGED SWORD, IT PENETRATES EVEN TO DIVIDING SOUL AND SPIRIT, JOINTS AND MARROW; IT JUDGES THE THOUGHTS AND ATTITUDES OF THE HEART.

HEBREWS 4:12

"Wow," he said as he studied the weapon. "An angelblade. Amazing!" The last weapon mentioned in Ephesians 6. And the main weapon of a warrior angel.

Jonah suddenly knew what he was supposed to do, why Michael had brought him here. Closing his eyes for a moment, he took a deep breath. He was ready. Glancing back one more time, he nodded toward the archangel, who met his gaze and then spread his great wings, sailing off of the cliff and out of sight.

Jonah looked back at the sword. Reaching out his hand slowly toward the hilt, he grabbed it, pulling it out of the tangled roots.

He felt a breath of wind, and when he opened his eyes, he was standing in the middle of the hospital basement again. His mother was kneeling there on the hard cement floor, eyes closed in fervent prayer. Eliza was still back against the wall, watching in stunned silence. The nephilim and the fallen ones were in front of him.

And Marduk was standing right there, exactly where he had been before they had disappeared. He saw Jonah and flinched.

Jonah looked down, and in his right hand, the silver sword blazed. It was long and razor sharp, but felt light in his hand as he turned it over. Marduk saw it, and the arrogance faded from his face.

"Angelblade? You?" he sputtered, dread etched across his face. "How did you . . . ?"

But before he could get the question out of his mouth, Jonah raised the sword over his shoulder and swung with everything he had.

The blade sliced through Marduk as his scream echoed through the room. He split in half and then disintegrated, and, like black snow, fell softly to the ground.

The horde of fallen angels stared on in shocked silence. Their commander was gone. Turned into dust by a thirteen-year-old kid.

Jonah reached down and extended his hand toward his mother. She grabbed it, and he pulled her to her feet. Eliza leapt up from against the wall and stood behind them.

The nephilim who had stared into Marduk's eyes began to look around at each other, as if they were unsure of where they were. They no longer looked like robots, ready to do whatever their leader commanded. Instead, they looked like lost, scared kids searching for someone to explain what was going on. Abaddon's power over them had been broken.

Jonah and his mother looked at each other and nodded. He turned to face the Fallen, glaring at them. They looked terrified and were already retreating. Yelling at the top of his lungs, he charged at them, his sword held high. Eleanor and Eliza followed close behind.

He swung at the first fallen angel he could find, and just as he did, a flash of light came from the direction that the fallen angels were running. Henry emerged from the tunnel, arrows flying, beating the retreating Fallen back toward them. Henry caught Jonah's eye and waved, smiling happily as he sent an arrow into the skull of one of the creatures, watching him turn to black dust.

Jonah swung the blade fiercely at the Fallen around him, the sword thudding into each one he met, causing them to evaporate. He knew they were not able to kill a being that could not die, but at least they could force them to disappear. The fallen ones were trapped between Jonah, Eleanor, Eliza, and Henry, and they were dropping and disappearing fast, their screams echoing off the cavern walls. Eleanor was throwing orbs of light right and left, her arm accurate and strong, and she looked like she was enjoying it. Eliza was moving back and forth, providing them protection with the shield of faith.

The fallen ones didn't have a chance. Out of the more than a hundred that had been there, only a dozen were left, and they scattered in all directions, disappearing into cracks and crevices, down the drain, looking for any way out that they could. Within seconds, they were all gone.

As Jonah held on to the sword and watched the last fallen angel disappear, his eyes were suddenly drawn across the room to a shadow moving quickly along the wall. He breathed in sharply, wondering if anyone else sensed what he did.

He felt an evil, raw power break across the room like a wave.

For the briefest of seconds, the shadow paused, and then took shape.

Long strands of stringy, dark hair covered almost the entire cheek of a pale face, so that only one eye was visible. One red, glaring eye looking to see who had taken an angelblade to his commander and destroyed his forces; to see who had ruined his careful plans.

Jonah knew in an instant who it was. Abaddon.

Then Jonah noticed that across his neck, he was missing a chunk of flesh. Like what an ax would do with one swipe to the base of a tree. The area was both crusty black, and bloody and raw. An old and an open wound.

Jonah felt the Evil One's gaze, searching. Fingers reaching inside his soul.

Finally, a cold whisper pierced him. "Who are you, to try and thwart my plan?" And then, as he continued to probe, "Ahh . . . a nephilim son. Well, *son of angels*, I am patient. And we will meet again."

His lips curled into a grin for the briefest of seconds, and then, as quickly as he had appeared, he snapped his hood up, covering both the scar and his head, and dissolved into a shapeless black shadow again. Slipping into the entrance of the underground tunnel, he was gone.

Jonah's legs suddenly felt weak, and he stumbled. He felt someone catch him, and he blinked and shook his head. It was his mom.

"Jonah," she said. "Oh, Jonah . . ." She held his face in her hands, looking deep into his eyes. "I thought Marduk had you. Like the others . . ." Eleanor began to weep. He wrapped his arms around his mother, closing his eyes as he felt his own happy tears coming. Eliza came running over and joined them.

"Okay, okay," he said after a few moments, beginning to get embarrassed by the hug fest. He shrugged his shoulders. "It was no big deal."

"No big deal, huh?" Henry said proudly. "Jonah says it's no big deal, Eleanor. You know, going toe-to-toe with Marduk and all of his fallen ones is just another day in the life of a thirteen-year-old."

"How is your father?" Eleanor asked Jonah and Eliza, then looked over at Henry.

Henry smiled. "He's probably pretty worried. He wanted to come after you, but Elohim had other plans. He'll be anxious to see all of us."

Eleanor closed her eyes and nodded. "And Jeremiah?"

"He's fine, Mom," said Eliza. "He doesn't have a clue—but I'm sure he misses you terribly."

"What about them?" Jonah said, glancing at the nephilim, who were wandering around and talking to each other in hushed voices.

"Their connection with Abaddon seems to have been broken," Henry said. "I'm not sure how much of a scar it will leave on them, however. Once we get them back home, I will send word to my fellow guardian angels to look after them with special care. I don't know if any of these people have even discovered their true origins. But something tells me we'll have a lot of explaining to do." He began to corral the nephilim and get them ready to move.

"Speaking of home, don't you think it's about time we got out of the hidden realm and went there?" said Eliza, looking up at her mom. "Together?"

With the nephilim behind them, they made their way back into the long tunnel and finally up through the castle floor. They climbed the narrow steps up into the tower.

When they were almost to the top, Jonah turned back to Eliza.

"Hey," he said, clearing his throat, "back there, in the basement. Did you . . . see him?"

She looked at him blankly. "Who?"

"You didn't see . . . ?" Jonah started. She squinted her eyes at him as they arrived at the roof. "Forget it. We can talk about it later."

Eleanor, Jonah, Eliza, and Henry stood for a while on the edge of the castle wall, looking at the park below and the skyscrapers just beyond. The sky was clear, the sun making its way down but still casting a warm glow.

"It's a nice afternoon for flying, don't you think?"

The voice came from behind them. They spun around to see Marcus and Taryn, the warrior angels, standing next to the seven other nephilim. A group of powerful-looking angels stood silently behind them.

"Marcus! Taryn!" Henry exclaimed. But then he folded his arms across his chest. "Where exactly have you all been?"

Marcus stepped forward, towering above him. "This was their mission, Henry, as you well know." His eyes twinkled. "And yours too."

Henry raised his eyebrows and said nothing, but couldn't hold back a grin.

Eliza tried to protest another angel ride, remembering the other she had taken earlier in the day. But she was too tired to put up much of a fight.

"I won't go too fast this time, Eliza," Henry promised. "And I'll fly in a straight line."

He held her hand and flapped his wings hard, and they shot off across the trees. Jonah heard her screams turn into distant laughter.

Eleanor held on to Taryn, and they gracefully dove over the edge. Jonah watched them climb, dark silhouettes against the brilliant light of sunset.

Jonah watched in awe as seven of the angels each took a nephilim in their arms and leapt off of the edge of the castle wall.

"Whoa!" he said. "Awesome!"

Marcus watched them for a minute too, and then turned to Jonah.

"What happened down there, what you did—" he said gruffly, "—well, Elohim was watching. And it was . . . impressive." Jonah managed a shy thanks as he looked down at his basketball shoes. The angel shared a few more words with Jonah, and then, holding on to his arm, they leapt together from the castle.

Jonah rode the wind all the way to Peacefield, on the arm of a warrior angel. It was cool and amazing, but all he really wanted to do now was go home.

EPILOGUE

PEACEFIELD

Jonah and Eliza walked along the path in the woods behind their house. Fall was here, but today it was unusually warm, the sun bursting through the grove of trees they walked underneath. Jeremiah was weaving in and out of them and the trees, having turned a large stick into a sword, battling imaginary villains.

If he only knew, Jonah thought.

It had been three days since they had flown back from New York City—by way of angel wing—with their mother. Henry had shown Jonah and Eliza how to leave the hidden realm when they touched down.

"It's just like going in," he'd said. "No special words or phrases. Just a heartfelt prayer to Elohim, asking to reenter the physical world. That should do it."

Jonah and Eliza had huddled together in the backyard, praying. When they opened their eyes, they saw the plain look of the trees, the grass, and each other—the shimmering glow invisible now—and knew they were back.

"I still can't believe it all," Eliza now said as they walked. "That Michael himself came and caught you, just at the right time, and gave you the sword."

They were still going over every event whenever they got the chance. "Look at this again," Jonah replied, pulling out the Bible from his pocket, the one from Mrs. Aldridge. "Ephesians 6:10–11: 'Finally, my brethren, be strong in the Lord and in the power of His might. Put on the whole armor of God, that you may be able to stand against the wiles of the devil.'" He closed the Bible and watched one squirrel chase another up a tree as they walked. "The only thing I can figure is that when I needed it most, I had a strength that was beyond my own. Elohim gave me His power and His armor."

Eliza began to nod her head. "When you wouldn't give in to Marduk, in your heart and mind you were saying that you would rather die than submit to him. And when you did that, you were letting go of your own strength and holding on to Elohim's."

Jonah patted his younger sister on the shoulder. "I don't think the fallen angels anticipated what two kids trusting in Elohim can do."

This didn't seem to comfort her, though. "You realize that Abaddon knows all about us now. And he's not going to be happy," she said darkly. "He won't give up that easily."

Jonah shook his head. "The nephilim have been delivered back to their families by the angels, safe and sound. Henry says they have all committed to becoming serious followers of Elohim. I guess who wouldn't, after a run-in like that with Marduk?"

"That is not exactly what I meant," she said. "I was talking about our family. You said that Marcus warned you. About how being a quarterling is an extremely rare thing, and that the things that happened in the hidden realm that day have never happened before. That Abaddon'll be on the warpath. We saw what his second-in-command could do."

She didn't have to say the rest. Her unsaid words hung heavily in the forest air. *Imagine what it would be like to face Abaddon himself.* Jonah had thought about that every day since he'd caught a glimpse of the Evil One's face.

Jonah thought about what Marcus had told him before they left the castle in Central Park. *"Being a quarterling in this world is a rare thing, Jonah. Danger will be around every corner. Learn to use your gifts. Always remember there is a war raging. Learn how to fight. You surely haven't seen the last of the Fallen."*

The words had stuck deep in his head that night, both exciting and troubling him. But one thought kept bubbling up. He whacked a stick lazily against the trees as they went along. "We have Elohim on our side, Eliza. What more do we need?"

They watched Jeremiah run around, hide behind the brush, and fire sticks at imaginary enemies.

"Come on, Jeremiah," Eliza called out. "You're going to make us late."

Soon they came to the clearing, underneath a canopy of oaks. Eleanor and Benjamin were perched on some large logs. They motioned for Jonah, Eliza, and Jeremiah to join them.

"I barely got to know Henry," muttered Eliza. "I can't believe he's going to be leaving us already."

"Cool!" Jeremiah said, pointing in front of them. "Real angels!"

Marcus and Taryn had stepped forward into the clearing and were now standing at attention, hands behind their backs. Henry was in the middle, dwarfed by them both.

"Um, you can see them, Jeremiah?" asked Jonah, with a raised eyebrow.

"Of course," he said, grinning and waving back. "I see all three of them. Don't you?"

Just then, old Mrs. Aldridge walked up. Jonah wondered if she was starting to lose her mind when she joined the angels and turned to face them, smiling serenely as if she were just taking an afternoon stroll. But then she began to transform before their eyes. Her hair was no longer bluish-gray and curly. Instead, it became long, shining like pure silver. The wrinkles in her skin disappeared. She stood up straight and tall. Wings shimmered into view on her back, full and brilliant white.

Jonah and Eliza looked at each other, too shocked to speak.

"Certainly after your time in the hidden realm, you now know that things aren't always as they appear to be, don't you?" she said to them, still smiling.

Before they could answer, another angel appeared in front of them, like he had walked out from behind an invisible curtain. He was covered with sleek metallic armor, and his wings were silver and looked as sharp as razor blades.

Jonah whispered, "Michael."

Marcus, Taryn, Camilla Aldridge, and Henry stood even taller and straighter now.

"Commander Michael, sir," said Marcus, bowing his head low.

"Michael?" Eliza whispered to Jonah. "As in, *archangel* Michael?"

Jonah nodded.

"Thank you, my dear friend," Michael said to Marcus, slapping him on the shoulder and turning to Mrs. Aldridge. He smiled slyly. "Camilla. Revealing your true colors today?"

She bowed her head low like Marcus. "It seemed like the right time, Commander."

Archangel Michael nodded crisply, then turned toward

Henry, who looked so ordinary and small next to the four angels beside him. "Let's get right to the point, shall we, Henry? I believe you've waited long enough for this."

Henry smiled shyly, stuffing his hands in his pockets.

"Friends of Elohim," said Michael, "it is not often that we confer upon any angelic being a promotion as we are today. But based on the heroic efforts above and beyond the call of duty by the guardian angel who stands before me today, and more importantly, because it is the will of Elohim, I am proud to promote you to Warrior-Class Angel, effective immediately."

Michael unsheathed a glowing silver sword from his belt and placed it in an awestruck Henry's hands.

"You will get your armor when you report for duty with the Second Battalion of the Angelic Forces of the West," he said, and extended his hand to Henry's. "Congratulations."

Jonah heard a roar of voices behind them, and he turned to see hundreds of angels standing and sitting in the trees. They were cheering for Henry.

"And you two," Michael said powerfully, pointing to Jonah and Eliza. "Come here."

They slowly rose from their seats on a tree stump and stood, heads bowed, in front of the archangel.

"Your bravery helped stop a worldwide tragedy from occurring," the angel said. "If the nephilim had been convinced to align themselves with Abaddon, the damage they could have done to the world, and to the cause of Elohim, would have been immense. The angelic host honors you for your courage in the heat of battle."

He shook both of their hands and turned them around to face their family. Benjamin, Eleanor, and Jeremiah beamed at them.

Jonah broke out into a huge grin. The angels raised their swords and arrows into the air, and cheered.

And as beams of sunlight broke through the trees and fell around them all, Jonah knew that Elohim was applauding too.

ABOUT THE AUTHOR

J erel Law is a gifted communicator, pastor, and church planter
with seventeen years of full-time ministry experience. He holds
a master of divinity degree from Gordon-Conwell Theological
Seminary and began writing fiction as a way to encourage his
children's faith to come alive. Law lives in North Carolina with
his family. *Spirit Fighter* is his first novel.

Learn more at www.jerellaw.com.

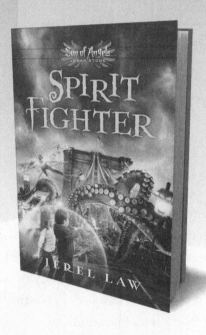

Travel back in time to London and solve mysteries with Sherlock Holmes's protégé!

Griffin Sharpe notices everything, which makes him the perfect detective! And since he lives next door to Sherlock Holmes, mysteries always seem to find him. With Griffin's keen mind and strong faith, together with his Uncle Rupert's genius inventions, there is no case too tricky for the detectives of 221 Baker Street!

By Jason Lethcoe

www.tommynelson.com
www.jasonlethcoe.com/holmes

Check out all of the great books in the series!

No Place Like Holmes ❖ *The Future Door*